ISLAND OF LOVE

ISLAND OF LOVE

Dorothy Lane

CHIVERS
THORNDIKE

This Large Print book is published by BBC Audiobooks Ltd, Bath, England and by Thorndike Press®, Waterville, Maine, USA.

Published in 2006 in the U.K. by arrangement with the Author.

Published in 2006 in the U.S. by arrangement with Dorothy Lane.

U.K. Hardcover ISBN 1–4056–3541–X (Chivers Large Print)
U.S. Softcover ISBN 0–7862–8185–5 (British Favorites)

The text of this Large Print edition is unabridged.
Other aspects of the book may vary from the original edition.

Set in 16 pt. New Times Roman.

Printed in Great Britain on acid-free paper.

British Library Cataloguing in Publication Data available

Library of Congress Cataloging-in-Publication Data

Lane, Dorothy, 1929–
    Island of love / by Dorothy Lane.
      p.   cm.
    "Thorndike Press large print British favorites."—T.p. verso.
    ISBN 0–7862–8185–5 (lg. print : sc : alk. paper)
    1. Large type books. I. Title.
    PS3562.O8388I85 2006
    813'.6—dc22   2005023637

CHAPTER ONE

'You did as I asked with your father's papers. You kept everything, Stella?'

'Yes. The whole lot has gone into store until I get back.'

'Good. Come down when you're ready. I'd like you to meet my nephew, Adam. He will be in charge of the diving operations on our expedition.'

'Very well, Sir James,' Stella replied as she prepared to follow the housekeeper upstairs.

'Call me James. Everyone does. We're a friendly crowd.'

Smiling, she nodded her agreement and followed the housekeeper. Although the woman was polite as she showed Stella to a room on the first floor, she had the impression that Sir James's housekeeper did not approve that she was taking the place of his usual secretary.

'I do hope Sir James's secretary is making a good recovery from her operation,' Stella said.

'I'm sure I don't know, Miss.' the woman replied, adding, 'I shall be serving afternoon tea in the lounge in half an hour.'

As the door closed, Stella flopped into a chair, wondering again if she had done the right thing in accepting Sir James's offer of a temporary job.

It was a pity that they had not met more recently but in the weeks before her father's death, the two men had been in contact and Stella knew her father was happy that the rift between the two friends had been healed.

With a start, she realised that she had been dreaming instead of getting ready to meet Sir James's nephew. Quickly she opened her case and took out a simple, loose-fitting blue dress and after a quick shower looked at herself critically in the mirror.

Since the death of her father, which had followed close on the heels of a broken love affair, she had lost weight. Her face had lost its childish roundness. She looked older, but it suited her. Quickly putting on a necklace and matching earrings, she made her way down the ornate staircase.

Sir James was writing when she entered the lounge so Stella went to the window seat and looked out onto the ornamental garden. A minute or two later, the housekeeper brought in the tea tray.

'Please help yourself, Miss,' she said quietly. 'Sir James doesn't like to be interrupted while he's working.'

Stella poured a cup of tea and took a freshly-baked scone. The phone rang abruptly and the housekeeper quickly answered it.

'It's your secretary, sir,' she said.

With a sigh of exasperation, Sir James thrust his papers aside and rose. 'I'll take it in the study.' he answered as he went out and banged the door. It was obvious he wasn't too pleased at the interruption.

'You were right about not interrupting Sir James when he's working,' Stella remarked, trying to make conversation with the housekeeper.

'You'd do well to remember it,' the woman replied as she left the room.

Stella was puzzled. She detected an air of disapproval and wondered what was wrong. It could just be that she was protective of her employer and resented those who might distract him from his work. Sir James soon returned, looking happy, and Stella felt more relaxed.

'How is your secretary feeling?' she asked as she poured the tea.

'Much better, thank you. She even thought that she might be fit enough to come out and join us.' He gave a self-conscious laugh. 'I have a problem with women—a problem common to many unmarried men. Several females that I know are very keen to put an end to my bachelor existence. My secretary, my assistant, Janet, even my housekeeper isn't too pleased about you coming to join us—I think she sees you as competition.'

Stella didn't reply. Nothing could have been further from her mind, but he was

3

distinguished with both a brilliant scientific mind and good looks so maybe he was being honest rather than boastful. And jealousy was probably the explanation for the housekeeper's attitude.

'It's time Adam was here,' he said, looking at his watch. 'He wants to talk about the diving equipment and we're going out to dinner this evening with Janet, my assistant.'

'Does your nephew always work with you?' Stella asked.

'No,' he replied quickly, 'only occasionally.'

As he spoke she saw a man standing in the doorway.

'Adam!' Sir James moved towards him, arms outstretched, which drew no response from his nephew. Adam was slightly shorter and broader than Sir James and had a thick shock of unruly dark hair and a slightly sullen expression. His old jeans and checked shirt contrasted sharply with his uncle's immaculate suit, white shirt and tie.

'And how is your mother these days, my boy?'

'She seems to be getting along fine, thank you, Uncle.'

'Good, it pays to get the best treatment available. Glad I could help.'

Stella sensed an undercurrent in this apparently innocuous conversation. There was some tension which she couldn't understand. The two men looked at one another, Sir

4

James's smile didn't seem to reach his eyes and Adam remained impassive. Stella, feeling her presence might be an embarrassment, was thinking about slipping away when her employer turned and drew her forward.

'Adam you must meet the latest member of our expedition. This is Stella who will act as our secretary on this trip. She's the daughter of an old friend of mine, Marcus Griffin, who died recently.

'You may remember I was telling you about some work we did together years ago on underwater equipment. And you will know some of the physics texts he produced for schools. He was an excellent teacher.'

Adam had a firm handshake and the most striking blue eyes Stella had ever seen. While Sir James oozed charm, his nephew gave a powerful impression of strength and determination.

'I wanted you two to meet before we have dinner with Janet tonight,' Sir James said as he put his arm possessively around Stella. 'And now, my dear, will you excuse Adam and me while we get on with some work. Please be ready by half-past seven.'

As Stella turned to leave, she saw a look of distaste on Adam's face. She felt angry. Why had her employer tried to infer that there was some bond of affection between them? She had a feeling that he was trying to annoy Adam, and seemingly he was succeeding.

Upstairs in her room, Stella stared out of the window into the garden below. The peace of the scene contrasted sharply with the chaos in her own mind. At first Sir James's offer of a job with his expedition had seemed a wonderful opportunity. But now she didn't feel quite so sure.

She hadn't met Sir James until after her father's death and, apart from his academic reputation, knew little about him. Maybe his gesture had been a rather clumsy attempt to show fatherly affection rather than an implication of some other kind of relationship between them.

But more than her employer's possessive attitude, the contempt in Adam's blue eyes filled her with embarrassment. After the trauma of losing her father and the upheaval of having to leave the family home, she told herself that maybe she was being over-sensitive.

She looked at her watch, realising it was time she should be getting ready for the evening outing. Dinner was to be an informal affair, so she took out a simple dress of dark green velvet which showed off her creamy skin and the auburn glints in her dark hair. When she went downstairs for half-past seven the look of appreciation on the faces of both men was obvious.

'You look charming, my dear, and so like your mother,' Sir James declared. Adam merely smiled his agreement. He had changed his clothes and looked very different, and much happier.

Before dinner they went to pick up Sir James's assistant, Janet, who had a flat at the university. She was waiting outside as they drew up in the car.

Sir James introduced her to Stella and after the briefest words of greeting, Janet turned her attention to Sir James, completely ignoring the others as she gave him a description of some complicated experiment on which she was working.

Adam turned to Stella, amusement in his eyes.

'You may have guessed, Janet is very dedicated to her work.'

She smiled her agreement and they sat back in companionable silence.

Janet was still talking as they parked the car and walked the short distance to the hotel. They had a drink in the bar before the meal, and Stella took stock of Janet. She was quite a plain woman but her conversation was obviously enough to keep Sir James interested for hours.

'I'll come into the laboratory tomorrow and have a look at what you're doing,' Sir James promised. 'But the idea tonight was to tell Stella something about the expedition and what we're planning to do. Come along Stella, my dear. We'll move to our table, I think.'

As he spoke, he took Stella's arm and left Janet to follow with Adam. When they were seated, Sir James was eager to get on with the business of the expedition.

'Everything's planned. There's nothing to discuss,' Janet retorted. 'I assumed your secretary was going to be well enough to accompany us. She's worked with you for some years now and knows our requirements. It wasn't a complicated operation—she should have been OK by now.'

'The heat could have caused problems and I felt it unwise to ask her to travel to an area where medical help was unavailable if any difficulties arose,' Sir James argued.

'We could send tapes back here for transcription—that has always formed the bulk of her duties,' Janet suggested.

'No—that wouldn't be satisfactory. What if something got lost on route? You know how unreliable the island post is.'

'I suppose you're right. Are you familiar with scientific terms, Stella?'

Before she could answer, Sir James said, 'Stella is the daughter of my dear friend, Marcus Griffin, who died recently. I have mentioned his work to you. She has worked on some of his physics textbooks, so has a good background knowledge.'

'Of course, the terms I use are mainly biological,' Janet told her.

The arrival of the meal provided a welcome

interruption and Sir James monopolised the conversation. He had a keen sense of fun and his anecdotes of previous expeditions were hilarious. Stella was amazed at how much time had passed when Janet decided they should think of leaving.

'Stella hasn't learned much about the trip,' Adam commented.

'Never mind. I can probably fill in all she needs to know.' Sir James smiled. 'The main thing was that I wanted us to have a little time together before we set off. It makes things easier when we're a small group. Do you feel you can bear to spend a few months in our company, Stella?'

'If you can stand my company, I'm sure I'll cope,' she replied with a smile.

*　　*　　*

The following morning, when Stella went down for breakfast, she found her employer had already eaten and left the house. She had just finished her meal when Janet arrived.

'Where has James gone?' she fussed. 'He knew I was coming. We haven't much time—and some decisions still have to be made. We can't just walk out and leave our research and our students.'

'I'm sorry, I don't know where he's gone. Can I give him a message, or is there anything I can do to help?'

'Thanks, but I don't think so. I'll have to get a move on. Ask him to ring me as soon as he returns.'

Stella decided to go upstairs and complete her packing, but before she could, Adam arrived.

He was looking for Sir James as well, but seemed happy to talk to Stella. Again she found his blue eyes very disconcerting and found herself slightly hesitant as she answered his questions about her father and his work.

'I hope it doesn't upset you talking about your father. I know you lost him recently and I guess at present it must be painful for you to think about the past.'

'I'm happy to talk about him. I'm sure he would have enjoyed meeting you, Adam.'

'I hope you don't mind me asking, but what is your relationship with my uncle?' he asked suddenly.

'He's very kindly employing me on a temporary basis,' she replied calmly, even though she was surprised at his question. 'After the expedition is over, I'll move on immediately and look for other employment.'

'James doesn't do things out of kindness. There's always a price to pay.'

'What do you mean? I'm being paid to do a job—as I assume you are.'

'I'm repaying a debt. I don't like working for my uncle, and hope this will be the last time.'

'But I thought you would have enjoyed

working with him.'

'Nobody works with him—you work for him, as many other scientists know to their cost,' Adam retorted bitterly. 'When he wants to block the work of someone else, it's easy to do—as I believe your father found out.'

'I know they were great friends at one time and then there was some sort of rift between them, but Dad never talked about it. I always thought they went their separate ways when my parents married and Dad decided to go into teaching. Your uncle wrote to my father after he learned Dad was ill.'

'Maybe I always see his worst side.' Adam sighed. 'But I don't want you to get hurt. And if Uncle James wants access to your father's work, please make sure he doesn't take advantage of you. Get some good advice before you hand anything over.'

Before Stella could reply, Sir James came in.

'Good morning Stella, my dear. I'm glad you were here to entertain Adam. And I caught up with Janet at the university—she said she'd been looking for me. While you're both here, I want you to hear the latest news. We're being joined by another colleague, Nigel Black.'

'You know I don't like working with Nigel.' Adam was obviously unhappy. 'He upsets the native divers, and he can cause a lot of trouble.'

'Adam, you promised to help me. You're in charge of the diving operation and Nigel will merely assist if you want him to do so. He will be doing his own work and is, after all, a member of the university staff.

'I've prepared an additional list of items we ought to take. Can you see to them, please?' Sir James added. 'I expect you'll want to spend as much time at home as possible before we go, so unless there are any problems, I'll see you at the airport.'

Adam took the list from his uncle, and left, an expression of anger on his face. Sir James laughed as the front door banged.

'Poor Adam! He tends to see everything in black and white. He can't recognise that most things are grey. I'm glad Nigel's coming, you'll like him. He's a very talented and charming young man. I think Adam's jealous because I took Nigel on as my research assistant. Adam's good at his job but he lacks drive and ambition. Nigel has both.'

'You're not afraid Adam will back out now?'

'No. He'll come round. He fell out with Nigel when we were on the island two summers ago. But I've recently organised some medical treatment for his mother—my sister—and he wants to repay me.'

Was it Adam's stubborn pride which made him insist on repaying the debt? Or was there some family conflict? While Adam resented the inclusion of Sir James's assistant in the

12

party, perhaps the presence of someone else might make things easier. As Stella reflected on the brilliant, mischievous leader of the expedition, the glowering Adam and the workaholic Janet, she fervently hoped that Nigel would be someone quite ordinary.

CHAPTER TWO

Stella eventually met Nigel when she and Sir James arrived at the airport. He was waiting with Janet and Adam and to Stella's relief they seemed to be on friendly terms. When Nigel greeted her, Stella was keenly aware of the admiration in his eyes.

A few hours later, they had finally reached their destination. The flight had been pleasant enough and Stella had been sitting beside Nigel, who turned out to be an interesting travelling companion.

Nigel took her arm as they left the plane.

'Let the old stuffed shirt listen to the boring Janet,' he replied when Stella protested that they were leaving their companions behind.

'And who are you calling a stuffed shirt?'

'Adam, of course. Our leader can be fun, but Adam is far too strait-laced. He might suit Janet and she'll probably settle for him when she finally realises she'll never catch old James—he's far too wily! I suppose you're not after James yourself?' He looked at her quizzically.

'Certainly not,' she retorted angrily.

'I was just curious, that's all. You are very attractive and James has always had an eye for

14

a pretty girl. Presumably that's why he's never tied himself down.'

Once they'd collected their luggage, they went to get a taxi from outside. Adam helped put the luggage in the boot, then after a couple of words with Sir James, began to walk away in the other direction.

'Isn't Adam coming?' Stella asked, watching his retreating figure.

'He's seeing that our equipment gets to the harbour for loading—we've some expensive gear and it needs taking care of,' Janet answered. 'It's nice to have someone to organise everything. He's very efficient and understands how to get things done here.'

Stella gasped at the brightness and colour as they sped on their way in the taxi. She had never seen anything like it before.

'It's just like a picture,' she breathed. 'It looks too good to be real.'

'Wait till you see our island,' Janet replied.

'And the coral reefs,' Nigel added. 'Teeming with the most beautiful fish you could imagine —to say nothing of the coral itself.'

When they reached the hotel Stella was glad to have a shower and lie down. A while later, Janet came in and advised her to get ready for dinner.

She had changed into a cotton dress which she wore with a rather odd wooden necklace. Stella put on a patterned cotton skirt and pale blue top. White beads and shoulder bag completed the outfit and she felt relaxed and refreshed.

After dinner, Nigel said he fancied a stroll and invited Stella to accompany him. She looked at Sir James, remembering that she was his employee now.

'Go ahead if you like, but don't be late. We've an early start tomorrow.'

'All right,' Stella said getting up. 'I'll probably sleep better after some exercise and it will be cooler now.'

'A good idea,' Adam said. 'I think we should all go out for a while. Coming, Janet?'

Janet nodded happily and looked hopefully towards Sir James.

'Count me out.' He smiled. 'This old man needs his rest. I'll see you all tomorrow.'

Stella saw the disappointment on Janet's face and cynical amusement in her employer's eyes as the four of them left.

'Let's try and shake off those two bores,' Nigel suggested as he seized Stella's hand.

'We can't be rude,' she whispered back. As she spoke Janet caught them up.

'Adam suggests we go to a little place we visited before—there's a steel band and a wonderful view of the bay.'

'But it's dark—we won't be able to see the bay,' Nigel protested.

'But the lights make it look wonderful,' Janet persisted 'It's a sight you'll never forget, Stella.'

'Stella's the one who hasn't been here before—let her choose,' Adam suggested. 'Would you like to have a quiet drink and look over the town to the sea, or would you like to go into town where it's lively and noisy?'

They all looked expectantly at Stella and she hesitated. She didn't want to look like she was taking sides.

'I think I'd quite like to hear the steel band and look across the bay.'

'That's agreed then,' Nigel replied cheerfully. 'Lead on, Adam.'

When they reached the hotel, Janet eagerly led them into the garden. 'Look,' she said.

Stella gazed in wonder at the twinkling pin-points of light stretching beyond them, high up the mountainside and spreading out below over the town and along the waterfront and the harbour like a spangled coverlet.

'It's absolutely beautiful,' Stella breathed.

The men went to get drinks while the women continued to marvel at the view. Although it was getting late, the night was warm and the soft breeze blew the perfume of flowers around them. Stella couldn't imagine a more beautiful scene. After an hour or so it was time to go back to the hotel.

'You and Janet go back if you like,' Nigel said. 'Stella and I will go inside for some dancing. We'll probably catch you up before you reach the hotel.'

'Why don't we all stay?' Adam put in

quickly. 'How about it, Janet?' But a floorshow had started when they went in. The four watched the dancers for a short time before making their way out through the crowd. Back at the hotel Janet attached herself to Stella, as their rooms were next to one another.

Nigel kissed Stella as they parted.

'See you tomorrow. We'll have a great time on the voyage.'

'It is an unwritten rule of the university,' Janet told her on the way to their rooms, 'that we don't have romantic involvements while we're on the island. It doesn't make for harmony.'

Stella glanced at Janet and realised she was being serious. She wondered if it was a rule that Janet had made up herself due to the lack of success she'd had with James. This trip was certainly proving to be interesting!

*   *   *

The following morning they were awakened early. Despite the hour, Stella was surprised to find how hot it was.

'When we get out to sea, the breeze will make it perfect,' Janet assured her.

When they arrived at the harbour, Adam saw to their luggage while the others went to their cabins. It was a cargo boat and Stella asked Janet how long the journey was likely to take.

'It all depends on the goods to be loaded on and off,' she said. 'It could be a couple of days. On the other hand, I've known it take a couple of weeks. Still, it gives us a chance to get acclimatised and then we can start work more quickly at the other end. Did you bring something to read?'

'Yes, but the cabin's a bit claustrophobic.'

'The lounge is fairly comfortable and you can always find a quiet spot on deck once we're at sea. Shall we go and explore?'

Stella nodded and the two went on a tour of the ship, eventually arriving on deck to see the last items being loaded and preparations made to cast off. She was surprised to see Adam helping the crew.

'Adam's very practical,' Janet commented. 'The sooner the loading is complete, the sooner we'll be on our way. And he'll be seeing that our equipment is stowed safely.'

'Our assistant is always inclined to interfere instead of leaving it to those whose job it is,' Nigel sneered, coming up behind them.

'Nonsense,' Janet retorted heatedly. 'Things always run smoothly, when he's around. We should be grateful . . .'

'It's all right, I was only teasing.'

As Janet turned and walked away, Stella noticed her usually pale face was flushed with anger.

'Janet's always had a soft spot for Adam,' Nigel muttered. 'They suit one another.'

19

Stella's discomfort must have shown because suddenly he smiled disarmingly.

'I'm sorry. That wasn't very kind, was it? I'll apologise to her later.' He tried to assume a penitent look but the glint of mischief in his brown eyes belied his contrition.

'I'm not feeling too good this morning,' he said. 'And it's all your fault.'

'My fault?' Stella queried in surprise.

'Yes. Sheer frustration. I wanted so much to spend last evening alone with you, showing you the town, and I didn't expect to have to take those two with us. Anyway, after you went to bed I tried to drown my sorrows. I should have had more sense. I need someone like you to look after me . . .'

The throbbing of the engines became louder and the shouting and activity of the crew increased, making it difficult to talk. Stella was glad to see Sir James appear.

'Ready for the off then?' He said, addressing the small group.

'I love being at sea.' Janet nodded, having come back on deck.

'Me too, normally,' Nigel put in. 'But at the moment I feel foul. I'm going below to take some aspirin. Sorry I was unpleasant just now, Janet. I've a filthy headache. You can probably guess the reason.'

'Oh, forget it.' Janet smiled. 'I'd go and lie down if I were you.'

With a rueful smile, Nigel went below deck

20

and the others stayed to watch as the ship moved slowly away and they felt the lifting motion as she turned into the open sea.

'I'm going to change into slacks in a minute,' Janet shouted to Stella.

'Yes, that's a good idea,' Stella agreed, but her words were blown away on the wind.

As they watched the white-crested waves and the bending palm trees on the now-distant shoreline, Adam joined them.

As she held down her wayward skirt. Stella reflected that he was the only one of the party who seemed to belong here. Sir James announced that he was going below and Janet turned to follow him. Stella was about to accompany them when Adam suggested that she might find the next hour or so interesting as she hadn't travelled to the island before.

'I was going to change into something more practical,' she explained.

'There's quite a sheltered spot along here, if you don't mind climbing over some of the gear,' he persuaded. 'But you might get a bit grubby—like me,' he added, holding up his hands.

'I don't mind that.' She laughed.

CHAPTER THREE

The following morning, breakfast was served early so they could get started quickly. Janet, James and Stella were just finishing when the housekeeper came in and hovered uncertainly on the edge of the group.

'I'm sorry to interrupt, sir,' she said nervously to James, 'but Thomas is here to see you and he seems very angry.'

'Did he say what was wrong?'

'No. He just said he's staying till he's seen you.'

'Thank you for telling me. I'd better not keep him waiting.'

'I can take Stella to see some of the artefacts we've brought up from the wrecks,' Janet suggested.

'Yes, I'd enjoy that.' Stella rose eagerly and the two went out together. As they left, she looked round and saw the imposing figure of Thomas glowering in the doorway at the other end of the room. He looked furious.

Sir James was walking towards him, and although almost as tall, he appeared pale and fragile beside the dark-skinned, muscular Thomas. Janet, too, looked back, noticing Stella's anxiety.

'Don't worry,' she urged. 'Whatever's wrong, James will sort it out. I'm sure it's nothing too serious.'

The two made their way to the laboratory which stood on its own, a little way from the main building. Stella did not quite know what she had expected to see, but she felt strangely disappointed by the odd-looking items over which Janet bent enthusiastically.

'These finds are amazing but as you know, it's the life around the reef which interests me. And, although I daren't breathe a word while we were still in touch with civilisation, we are on the verge of recording a real discovery.

'There's a form of life here which we thought was extinct. Of course the discovery must remain an absolute secret until our material is published. It will be sensational.'

'It all sounds fascinating,' Stella remarked.

'It is,' Janet replied. 'Tell me, are you familiar with word processors?'

'Oh yes. I used one when I worked at the school.'

'Good. We can start cataloguing some of our finds. I was holding off until the list was complete, but with the computer we can insert bits all the time.'

While Steve waited outside for Janet to lock up. Sir James and Thomas emerged from the building opposite. They were talking seriously.

Suddenly Stella was aware that the attention of the two men was on her, Sir James still talking emphatically and Thomas staring. Then suddenly Thomas smiled, the two men shook hands and Thomas loped away.

By the time Janet emerged from the laboratory he was gone and Sir James had returned indoors. Stella planned to ask Sir James what had been going on, but when they got to the house he had already gone for his siesta.

The evening was taken up with a discussion of the equipment they would need the following day. Clearly Janet knew exactly what she wanted and she and Adam soon had the expedition organised. Afterwards, Sir James took Nigel off for a private discussion, leaving Janet and Adam sorting out a few minor details.

It was a long time before Sir James and Nigel returned. Stella looked up from her book as they entered and noticed that the older man looked angry, and his face was flushed.

Nigel, on the other hand, was looking very guilty. Sir James appeared anxious to cover up any sign of strained relations but his jovial demeanour seemed somewhat forced.

'Join us for a drink, Stella,' he urged. 'Nigel—get some glasses. And what about you, Janet? Do you intend to talk about work all night?'

Janet had seemed deeply engrossed in her conversation with Adam, but stopped immediately. Adam went to help Nigel with the drinks while the other three moved out on to the patio.

After a while, Sir James asked Stella to take a stroll with him. Taking her arm, he guided her towards the bay where the water sparkled black and silver under the moon. He reminisced about the years gone by, and the love he had had for Stella's mother, which Stella had known nothing about.

'I suppose she never mentioned me?' he queried.

'No, I don't remember that she did.' Stella could barely hide her surprise.

'I can't describe my grief at not only losing her love and friendship but also the friendship of my best friend—your father. I know the better man won, but the pain always remains.'

This was all news to Stella—and she couldn't help wondering why Sir James was choosing to tell her.

'Stella,' Sir James broke in on her thoughts. 'I hardly like to ask you—but would you accept something I once bought for your mother? It would make an old man very happy. I never parted with the ring I intended for her and it's not of any great value but I'd like you to have it . . .'

After a few minutes' thought, Stella decided to accept the gift, although she couldn't help thinking Sir James was being over-dramatic. There was something a little false about his

25

behaviour.

'I'll give you the ring tomorrow. I hoped I would find the courage to speak to you about it and I'm glad you've decided to accept it.'

Stella felt a sense of relief as they began to stroll back to join the rest of the party. However her contentment was shattered as she saw the look of anger on Janet's face and Adam's stony expression.

'I'm going to bed,' Janet muttered, her voice shaking. 'Goodnight.'

'Me, too.' Adam said as he picked up Janet's bag and tenderly draped the light shawl round her shoulders. As he turned to say goodnight to the others, Stella was aware of the smouldering resentment behind his polite words. With a wry smile Sir James followed after them.

'I bet you're ready for another drink,' Nigel said as he moved towards the kitchen. 'What would you like? Something with lots of ice?'

'No. It's time I went to bed, too. I'm really tired,' Stella said wearily.

'But we're on our own now, we've got a chance to talk.'

'No, I really am tired, and I've got a headache. I expect it's the sun.'

'But I'd like to chat for a while. Please don't go,' Nigel begged.

'We've got plenty of time to talk in the coming weeks.' She laughed as she removed his restraining arm, and left.

26

*   *   *

Stella had been a bit worried about meeting Janet the following morning, but she was back to her usual self. She was going out to the reef with Adam and leaving some work for Stella to do. Nigel had returned to bed complaining of a headache.

'I think he over-indulged last night,' Sir James said. 'And there's a lot to get through today. But first, Stella my dear, I must give you something. It's in my office and I want to have a private word with you.' He led her through to a small room and closed the door. 'I feel rather awkward asking you to do this, but I'd regard it as a great kindness if you'd help us . . .'

'I will if I can,' she said cautiously.

'Do you remember when Thomas came over to speak to me yesterday?'

'Yes.'

'Unfortunately he was very upset. It seems that Nigel and Adam broke our rules on their last visit here by getting to know a couple of the local girls. I knew nothing about it until now. They shouldn't have done it—for one thing, our cultures are completely different . . .' He paused.

'But how can I help?'

'One of the girls, whom Nigel was seeing, is now married to Thomas. Not only is Thomas

27

still angry about Nigel's behaviour but he also fears it may be repeated. And we don't want to do anything which might jeopardise our relationship with the islanders.

'Thomas is an island leader. He is also the best diver, and a very able man. If he is offended we could end up without any help from the native population. We could well be denied access here in the future . . .' He sighed heavily. 'I said the only thing I thought would reassure him. I told him that Nigel was to be married to a girl from his own country . . .'

'But what has that got to do with me?' Stella asked, her heart already sinking.

'I would like you to let everyone think you and Nigel are to be married. It will help us out of a difficult situation and I'd be tremendously grateful. I wouldn't ask, but we can't afford to ruin our future on the island.'

'Why not ask Janet? They've been friends for a long time—it would seem a natural thing when they have similar interests.'

Her employer laughed nervously.

'People here know that Janet has feelings for me so I'm afraid they wouldn't believe that she could be engaged to another man.'

'What about Adam—if he's been too friendly with the native girls isn't he going to need a fiancée too?'

'Fortunately, there are no angry young men on his trail,' Sir James replied. 'So, Stella, if you could do this for me I'll be extremely

28

grateful.'

It was clearly an instruction rather than a question and without waiting for Stella to reply, he produced a box from his pocket.

'Try this for size.' He took her left hand and slipped a ring on her finger.

It fitted perfectly and was a lovely piece of jewellery—a ruby surrounded by diamonds. But Stella still didn't feel especially comfortable with the situation.

'Do you like it?' he asked at length, still holding her hand.

'It's lovely,' she admitted. 'But I don't know if . . .'

'Don't worry, Stella,' her employer urged. 'I've pointed out to Nigel the error of his ways and I've told him of my regard for you and reminded him that it's my ring you'll be wearing.'

Stella felt even more bewildered. The situation was becoming increasingly complicated and she wasn't sure if she could cope.

'You don't look well, my dear,' James said. 'Is the heat bothering you?'

'No, I'm fine.'

'I don't suppose you've got too much work to do yet?'

'No, just a few things Janet gave me before she left for the reef.'

'Then why not go and have a swim before it gets too hot. You can always work later in the day.'

'That sounds like a good idea,' she replied coolly as she turned to leave.

'Thank you so much for this.' James kissed her hand. 'I can't tell you how important this is to me.'

Escaping to her room, Stella put on her bikini and covered it with a towelling tunic. Packing a towel and sun tan lotion into her bag, she hurried away. It was only when she reached the sea that she remembered she was still wearing the ring. She was reluctant to keep it on in case it slipped from her finger. Still, it would be safe in the bag.

The water was warm and surprisingly shallow. Stella swam lazily, turning on to her back and floating, eyes closed, revelling in the sunshine. She had covered quite a distance when she eventually looked back. She left the sea for a few minutes and rested on the soft, white sand. She had thought of walking back along the beach but the water was much more inviting.

Eventually she reached the place from which she had set off and was looking forward to a shower when she got back to the house. But when she went to collect her bag from underneath a palm tree, she found it had disappeared.

Stella looked around but there was nothing and no-one in sight and the bright tunic and bag had disappeared. Had someone been watching her—waiting until she went for a swim? Suddenly her heart sunk. Sir James's ring was in the bag. And now it was gone.

Stumbling a little in the shimmering brightness she made her way back to the house. When she reached her room, she showered and applied lotion to her red skin. It seemed sensible to go to the beach later and search for her belongings. It would be best to have a rest, complete the work Janet had left, then return when the sun was less strong.

But the exercise must have exhausted her. She fell into a deep sleep and was awakened by someone opening her bedroom door.

'It's all right. She's here,' Janet called to the others.

Stella fought off the mists of sleep and struggled into a sitting position.

'You had us all worried sick. Stella. Adam is down at the beach searching for you. I've sent someone to tell him you're safe.'

'What have I done?' Stella asked in bewilderment.

'Left your dress and bag by the water's edge, they're wet through. I've brought them up. We thought you'd gone swimming and had an accident. Adam was absolutely frantic. Didn't it occur to you that anyone who found your things would be worried about you?'

'But I didn't leave my things by the edge of the sea. I left them in the shade of the trees. When I returned from swimming they'd gone.'

'What do you mean—gone?'

'They'd disappeared!'

Janet looked puzzled.

'I suppose some of the children could have been playing around although they wouldn't normally touch anything that belonged to us. Did you see anyone?'

'No. No-one at all.'

'Well, here are your things. Is everything there?'

Stella put aside her dress and removed the contents of the bag. The sun-screen lotion and sandals were there but the now-soggy handkerchief in which she had wrapped the ring was empty.

'The ring,' she said, searching the bottom of the bag 'It's gone! It was in my handkerchief but it's not there now.'

'It must be. Are you sure you didn't drop it?' Janet demanded.

'No. It was definitely wrapped in the handkerchief.'

'Then someone must have taken it. We'll have to tell James. Our meal's ready anyway—so come on.'

'You go, Janet—I'll be along in a minute.'

Stella felt dreadful. She didn't relish having to tell her employer she'd been careless enough to lose the ring but taking a deep breath, she went through to the dining room.

To her complete astonishment the incident which had caused her so much worry was

32

dismissed quite briefly. Sir James told her not to worry so much and it would be found eventually.

He seemed to regard the loss of the ring as inconvenient rather than distressing and Stella wondered if he had told the truth about it.

'Now we know you are safe, my dear,' he said, 'we can all toast Janet's success. She has taken some remarkable pictures today—pictures which will shake the scientific world!'

'Adam did a lot of work, too,' she said, flushing with pleasure. 'I couldn't have managed without him.'

'But the discovery was yours and you deserve all the credit,' Adam said.

'When you've all finished displaying your undoubted modesty,' Nigel, put in, 'you'd better get down to practicalities. You're going to want that lot developing quickly to make sure they're OK.'

'Nigel's right. We can't run any risks with pictures like that,' Sir James said. 'They'll have to be developed professionally before we leave the island. And of course, we don't want our discovery leaking out before we've got the whole thing ready for publication. You'll have to take them on the next boat, Janet. Stay while they're developed and bring them back with you.'

'It's difficult for me. The technicians we're using are French-speaking—and my French isn't good. Couldn't someone else go?'

'I need both Nigel and Adam—we're examining wrecks and testing our new equipment from tomorrow, sea conditions permitting. And time is precious. Stella, how's your French?'

'Not too bad—I can get by quite well.'

'That's great! You can both leave on the next boat. It's better for two of you to go— you'll probably have to wait for a ship coming back this way, so you can have a few days' holiday.'

'The mail boat will possibly be here tomorrow,' Adam warned. 'So you'll have to be ready.'

After dinner, Stella went into the office to type out some letters for Sir James. She raised the blinds and opened the window in the stuffy room.

She secured it then started work. She had just completed the last letter and was covering the machine when she heard a noise outside. Thinking it was Sir James coming to see how she was getting on, she turned towards the door, carrying the letters. Behind her, there was the crash of shattering glass and something heavy hit the floor. Stella screamed, although she was sure she could hear someone running away.

She hardly dared to breathe as the door was flung open. To her relief it was Adam who appeared.

'Are you all right?'

'I'm fine but someone smashed the window. I heard them running away.'

Gently moving her aside, he went to examine the missile which had shattered the glass.

'A piece of rock,' he said, sounding puzzled. 'We usually leave the blinds down.'

'If I'd known someone was going to throw a rock through the window, that's exactly what I would have done,' Stella said sarcastically.

'It's mainly so that we don't attract attention to the things we have here. The islanders are very poor, although their standard of living has improved since we came but it wouldn't be fair of us to put temptation in their way.'

'In that case, why did the person run away if their intention was to break in and steal something?' Stella protested.

'What's this?' As Adam spoke he went across the room, treading warily to avoid the broken glass. Stooping, he picked up something which glittered and held it out on the palm of his hand.

'The ring I lost!' she exclaimed.

Sir James and Nigel had appeared in the doorway and the older man stepped forward and took the ring from Adam.

'Allow me, my dear.'

He replaced the ring on Stella's third finger, putting an arm around her as he spoke to Adam.

'Obviously someone was looking for an

35

opportunity to return the ring. It's a pity whoever it was couldn't have found a more suitable way. However Stella can now wear the ring which tells the islanders she's engaged to Nigel. Only we know that the ring was my gift.'

'I'll clear away this glass, if you like,' Adam said, his face expressionless.

As they returned to the house, Stella remembered she had left the letters behind.

'I'll get them,' Nigel offered.

'No. I know where left them,' Stella insisted as she hurried back.

Adam was fixing a large piece of board in the broken window. He turned as she entered, but there was no welcoming smile on his face.

'I've just come back to collect the letters,' she explained. 'I put them down when you picked up the ring.'

'Yes, of course. I know how upset you were about losing it.' He sighed loudly. 'This all seems very unjust to me—here you are playing at being engaged to Nigel, while being involved with my uncle. It seems I don't get a look in anywhere.'

Stella managed a faint smile as she picked up the letters and fled. Tears filled her eyes as she hurried to her room, hoping she wouldn't meet anyone. She had no idea that Adam felt anything for her—he had always been friendly but she hadn't suspected anything. Which was why she had been denying her feelings for him all along.

And he was right about Sir James. He kept suggesting that there was something between them, which wasn't what Stella wanted at all.

Her thoughts were interrupted as Janet knocked on the door and asked about James's letters.

'Come in, Janet. They're here. I'm just about to wash my face. Do my eyes look very red?'

'Just a bit, but you've had a few shocks today. I'll take the letters for you then you can lie down for a while. A few days away from here will do you the world of good. Can I get you a drink and some aspirin?'

'No, it's all right. I'll just have a rest if you'll take the letters for me.'

When Janet left, Stella tried to compose herself. She had to admit that she had been attracted to Adam at their first meeting but she had only been thinking about her job then and had no desire to rock the boat.

Afraid that her absence would cause someone to come looking for her, Stella decided it would be best to join the others. There were some letters she ought to write and hopefully she would be able to avoid having to talk to Adam or his uncle. However, to her relief, only Janet was sitting in the lounge.

She, too, was writing letters, but insisted on breaking off to bring supper for herself and Stella. She was very concerned about Stella's unpleasant experience and assured her that such a thing had never happened before and was most unlikely ever to happen again.

When Stella finally got down to her letter-writing, she reflected that there was a very kind side to Janet's nature.

CHAPTER FOUR

The following day Stella woke early. She had packed the few things needed for the journey and hoped she and Janet would be able to leave soon.

Even the company of Janet would be more welcome than that of the male members of the party. She looked through the slatted blinds of her bedroom window, hoping to see some sign of the ship's arrival.

As she was about to turn away she saw Adam in the distance. There was someone with him—a native girl in a brightly-coloured dress.

As Stella watched, the two parted. The girl disappeared into the trees while Adam came out of the grove and walked towards the sea. She felt a stab of jealousy and remembered Sir James's remarks about the behaviour of Nigel and Adam on an earlier occasion. Surely Adam wouldn't be taking such risks again?

At breakfast, Stella was told that the boat had not yet arrived, and that weather conditions reported on the radio meant it would be unwise to sail beyond the reef.

'The sea doesn't look too rough,' Stella commented. 'I was watching it from my window this morning.' She looked at Adam as she spoke, wondering if he would realise he might have been seen with the girl, but he didn't even look up.

'It's very sheltered this side of the reef,' Sir James said. 'But the particular wreck I want to look at is in slightly deeper water a good way out on the other side.

'I found it when we were here two years ago and suspect that the sea had only recently thrown it up.'

'I don't feel I can settle down to work,' Janet remarked. 'I'm so anxious to get the pictures developed and to know they're OK. I can still hardly believe what I saw.'

'I'm sure they'll be great,' Adam told her. 'And the general opinion seems to be that the boat will arrive tomorrow, so you won't have long to wait. There's a party tonight and we're all invited. It's a leaving party. Winston travels on the same boat as you—he's going to his new school. And two of the older girls are going to do a pre-nursing course . . .'

'I know all about it,' Sir James interrupted. 'Thomas is accompanying them. He has a strong sense of duty to his family and to all the children of the island. Winston is his brother and the parents of the girls are happy that he will take care of them as well. These children have seen nothing of the world beyond their own island. They need someone to look after them.'

'I can't see why some other adult couldn't take on the job.'

'We ought to attend the party,' Janet said quickly. 'The islanders will appreciate it.'

'Of course we'll go,' Nigel said. 'Or at any rate, Stella and I will go. We can dance the night away on the beach under the moon. As my fiancée you'll be expected to dance only with me.'

'We'll all igo,' Adam retorted. 'But Janet and Stella won't want to dance all night if they're travelling tomorrow.'

The two girls agreed with him and Sir James said reluctantly that if the others were going he ought to go, too.

'I'll take you out in our boat this morning, Stella,' Nigel said. 'You've been slogging away here while we've been out in the sun on the reef.'

'We can all go,' Sir James interrupted. 'As we're not going far we can use the smaller boat. We can manage that ourselves, though I had hoped to be taking the bigger boat out to get on with my own work. We'll just have to hope conditions are right when Thomas deigns to return to his duties.'

When the girls reached the boat half an hour later. the men were already there, Adam waiting to cast off Stella, stepped aboard carefully as Adam steadied the boat with his foot while taking her arm. Janet followed and once they were both safely on, Adam released the rope. Nigel opened the throttle and the vessel shot away from the jetty.

Eventually they dropped anchor in the shallow water over the reef. Adam came to sit by Stella while Janet and Sir James were engrossed in a private discussion.

'Look.' Adam touched Stella's arm and pointed towards a break in the coral and she became aware of tiny brilliantly-coloured fish.

'Butterfly fish,' Adam told her. 'And look—there's an angel fish. They're very shy and tend to disappear as soon as a diver goes down.'

She glanced up from the fascinating scene under the water and saw Adam look towards his uncle.

'How far out does your wreck lie?' he asked. 'If it's not too far we might be able to have a look at it.'

'No—it's much too far out. We can't get to it in this boat today.'

'Exactly where is it?' Adam demanded. 'If I'm going to organise the dive I have to know where we're going.'

'We'll have to do a survey before we plan the dive, so you'll see it then.'

'Where is it?' Adam repeated in a voice that brooked no argument.

Sir James turned towards the small cabin and Adam followed. Stella could feel the tension mounting. She sensed that both Nigel and Janet were uneasy. She wasn't surprised to hear Adam's voice raised in anger.

'You won't get Thomas to dive there. You know about the fishing boats which were dashed to pieces in that very place—including his father's boat. The islanders have never fished that area since.

'Besides. the currents can be treacherous—and the shelf extends only a short distance. It's a dangerous place. What's special about this wreck? There are others in safer and more accessible places.'

'The natives' superstitions will soon disappear if you offer them a good reward,' Nigel sneered, as the two emerged from the cabin. 'Make them an offer they can't refuse. We usually pay them peanuts, don't we?'

'I don't think a lot of extra money is a good idea,' Adam replied. 'We don't want to put lives at risk. No wreck is worth it.'

'Are you scared of the job? Are you backing out after promising to help me?' Sir James demanded.

'No. But neither am I foolhardy.'

'There's no need to take unnecessary risks,' Sir James retorted. 'This will be just a job like any other and surely Thomas and his people owe us something—we've done a great deal for them. But there's no need to mix today's pleasure cruise with business.'

A look of anger at his uncle's patronising tone showed briefly on Adam's face, but without answering he started the engine and moved slowly along the reef and in a wide arc towards the distant jetty. When they arrived at the villa it was almost time for the afternoon siesta. No-one spoke much as they ate and Stella was glad to escape to her own room to lie down.

When she awoke she decided to go into the lounge and read a book so that she could distance herself from any arguments which might be taking place. However, only Janet was there and she put her own book down when she saw Stella.

'I was wondering what to wear for the party tonight.' Stella said, keen not to be drawn into a discussion on the day's events.

'There's no need to dress up—just a cotton dress or a skirt and top—the brighter the better.'

Soon Adam joined them. He seemed relaxed and friendly, but managed to steer the conversation round to the subject of the wreck.

'I'm sure there'll be no problems,' Janet told him. 'You're capable and experienced and the others trust your judgement.'

'Have you seen it yourself, Janet?'

'No. I shall see it for the first time when you do—if it's still there. I must go and load my camera to take some pictures at the party tonight.'

Janet departed and Adam watched her go, a puzzled look on his face. 'There's something odd about this wreck,' he said quietly. 'Something that everyone except me seems to know. Has James said anything?'

'No. I know nothing except what I overheard on the boat this morning.'

'It's going to be difficult getting Thomas to dive there—or even getting the crew to sail the boat to that area.'

It was dark when the small group crowded into a battered jeep and set off for the party. Earlier, Dominique, the housekeeper, had left with a large quantity of food.

'We could do with seatbelts in here,' Janet remarked to Stella as they drove away, with Nigel sitting between the two girls at the back.

'I'd settle for springs,' Nigel said. 'Or better still, a new vehicle.'

Eventually they heard sounds of music and laughter and as Adam eased the car gently down a slope, a wide bay came into view. The huge moon was eclipsed by the lights strung between poles and the fires over which food was being cooked. Stella was amazed at the amount of people there.

'Some of them will have travelled a long way to be here,' Janet told her. 'The party will go on till daybreak and then they'll start the long trek home. Come and taste some of the fish—it's delicious.'

Lots of people crowded round, introducing themselves and offering refreshments to the visitors. In the background were the strains of the steel band and above the noise Stella heard Winston asking for help with some

45

lighting problem.

Adam followed the boy, as did Janet and Sir James. Stella went too, and it was only when they had threaded their way through the friendly crowd and reached the place where Thomas was examining a string of flickering lights, that she realised Nigel wasn't with them.

'I've lost Nigel!' Stella exclaimed, remembering that as his fiancée. she would be expected to accompany him.

'Don't worry,' Adam told her. 'Stay here— he'll find you.'

'He should take care of you—as I take care of my wife,' Thomas said. 'Charity, meet Stella.' As he spoke, he drew forward a tall, slim girl who had been standing in the shadows. Charity gave a smile but looked rather uneasy. She told them she would go and bring food for them.

'We'll come with you,' Janet said, and the three women went to collect plates of food. Stella was sure that this was the girl to whom Adam had been talking that morning. Was that the reason for her uneasiness?

When they returned with food, the lights were fixed and the group settled down by the band to listen.

Later, they joined a throng of dancers. Only Sir James remained aloof, watching the celebrations from a distance.

During a lull in the music, Stella wandered away from the dancers to remove her sandals and shake out the sand. She seated herself by the trunk of a palm tree and rested for a few moments, feeling the soft warm breeze caressing her. Suddenly she heard Adam's voice nearby.

'I made you a promise and I haven't broken it. You must trust me.'

There were sounds of movement and Adam and Charity emerged from the trees a short distance away. Stella wished she had not overheard the snippet of conversation.

She replaced her shoes and was about to join the dancers again when Thomas loomed up in front of her.

'Why are you not with your fiancé?' he demanded.

'I lost him soon after we arrived—I don't know where he is.'

'The ways of your country are different from ours. If I had neglected Charity in such a way she would have been extremely angry.'

Stella smiled, not knowing what to say, and thankful that by now Adam and Charity would have lost themselves in the crowd, escaping notice.

'Have you seen Adam?' he asked. 'I must speak with him.'

'I think he passed a few minutes ago when I was tipping the sand from my shoes. He didn't notice me. He went that way.'

'In that case, I will find him. I am sorry to tell you that your fiancé has drunk too much

47

and is becoming a nuisance. If I approach him I might lose my temper. I do not want to cause unnecessary trouble, or to upset you.' As he spoke, Stella noticed her employer coming towards them.

'Here's James. He'll speak to Nigel.'

'There is only one in your party who understands and can help. I will find Adam. And I warn you—if you love your man, you must watch over him and look after him. He will always need your strength because he is weak.'

Thomas turned and hurried away and Stella hoped fervently that Adam and Charity had parted company.

'What's the trouble?' Sir James demanded. 'Thomas looks quite murderous!'

'He thinks Nigel has had too much to drink and he's looking for Adam.'

'Hysterical natives!' her employer muttered in disgust. 'And why didn't you stay with Nigel? You're supposed to be engaged to him.'

'I agreed to that charade only for your convenience,' Stella said angrily. 'I didn't realise acting as nursemaid to your assistant was part of my duties. If it was, you should have made it clear from the start.' Glaring at him, Stella walked off to join the crowd.

It was some time later that Winston told her the others were ready to go. As she turned away from the dancers she realised that she was very tired.

'Where's Nigel?' she asked Janet as they drove away.

'Don't worry about him. Adam got him sobered up and took him back to the villa. Nigel can be an idiot sometimes.'

'He finds these stupid native junketings as boring as I do,' Sir James snapped. 'He has my sympathy on this occasion.'

Stella was content to forget the incident which had marred an enjoyable experience. But when she went to bed, the memory which remained with her was that of Charity and Adam furtively emerging from the shadows.

CHAPTER FIVE

The following morning, word came that the vessel had arrived. Stella couldn't have been more pleased.

Adam was to take them to the harbour and Stella was surprised at his patience as Janet flapped and panicked trying to get ready.

'These films are so important to Janet,' Adam explained while he and Stella waited for her in the jeep. 'She lives for her work so I'm not sure how she'll take to having a few days off. But she could do with relaxing a bit.'

'I'll do my best to see Janet enjoys the break,' Stella assured Adam.

When Janet finally rushed back to the vehicle, she insisted that Stella should sit in front with Adam while she went behind with the luggage and held the precious films.

When they reached the ship, Adam carried their bags aboard, laughing as Janet refused to entrust the films to him. Once in their cabin, she stowed them away and seemed calmer. They went on deck and saw Thomas and Charity arriving with Winston and the girls who were going away to school.

The ship was soon ready to leave and Adam kissed Stella and Janet. Stella felt her heart pounding at his touch, especially as his arm remained round her until the final call came for those who had to leave. Thomas and Charity were still holding each other and Adam laughingly dragged Thomas's wife down the gangway and stayed beside her on the quay.

Stella stood watching and waving as the shoreline grew fainter. Adam and Charity, still standing at the quay were the last people she could see. She saw a large shadow blocking out the sunlight and realised that Thomas was standing beside her.

'Your man did not come to see you leave,' he remarked. 'Surely he should have wanted to know you were safely aboard.'

'I don't think he's feeling very well this morning.'

'That is no excuse. Our girls would not be happy with such behaviour. Here, we all care for one another. Adam behaves like one of our people. I was happy to leave my wife with him. He is a good man.'

Stella hoped fervently that this was true although she reflected uneasily that there had been those furtive meetings between the two of them.

She was saved from further conversation when Janet came over, accompanied by the two girls and suggested that as it was getting very hot and everyone must be feeling tired after last night's party, it would be a good idea to go below and have a rest.

After a couple of hours rest, Stella woke to find Janet had gone. She eventually found her in the lounge, playing games with Winston and the two girls, watched by Thomas.

'They all seem to be having a good time,' Stella remarked to Thomas.

'They are making the most of their journey. When they reach school, there will be much hard work for them. But they know this is a great opportunity their parents never had and they will do their best.'

Later, the party went on deck where Thomas and Janet pointed out various landmarks and answered the children's incessant questions. Thomas seemed to know as much as Janet about life beneath the sea and led the party round the ship as he explained the function of various pieces of equipment. His expertise seemed to suggest experience far beyond the confines of his small island.

Stella mentioned her surprise at the breadth of his knowledge when they retired for the night.

'Yes, he is a most intelligent man,' Janet agreed. 'And he's doing a wonderful job on the island—persuading people to make use of technologies which suit their needs.

'And, of course, he knows their needs in a way no outsider could. He feels he has the advantage of useful knowledge from other parts of the world without the accompanying greed and selfishness we so often see. They're very close, family-oriented people on the island.'

'He told me he finds it difficult to understand our people,' Stella said. 'He feels Sir James and Nigel should have accompanied us aboard. He seemed so angry about Nigel last night, I wouldn't have thought he'd have wanted to see him. And probably James was quite anxious to keep out of his way as well.'

'I've known Thomas for a long time,' Janet told her. 'His temper is easily aroused—and he knows it. But he is very fair. We have had problems with Nigel before, I thought he would have learned his lesson.

'It was James's intention to read the riot act to him as soon as we'd left. Hopefully after we've completed the present business, we can get on with the other job. When Nigel's actually working, he's all right. Unfortunately he has a low boredom threshold.'

Stella noticed that there had been no mention of Adam's behaviour causing problems, and Thomas seemed to have a good opinion of him, yet Sir James had said that both his assistants had been too friendly with island girls. Was Janet shielding Adam, of whom she was clearly very fond, or perhaps she didn't know the full story?

'Thomas seemed happy to leave his wife with Adam,' she remarked.

53

'Yes they've a good understanding and Thomas knows that if there are any problems, he will take care of them. Last time Nigel was here he became too friendly with Charity. Not having the sophistication of our society she believed he intended to marry her and take her away to a wonderful new life. She jilted poor Thomas who adored her and she was devastated when Nigel left without her.

'Fortunately she and Thomas were reconciled and it all ended happily. But Thomas was not pleased to see Nigel back again and I don't suppose she was either. They feel Nigel has abused the island's hospitality.'

'I'm surprised James encouraged him to come back,' Stella remarked. 'And if Nigel gets so bored here, why did he want to come?'

Janet seemed to be hesitant for a moment.

'James thought he might need him if the job he has in mind proved difficult—or if Adam became awkward . . . Adam might well refuse to do something if he felt the risk was too great. Nigel is more like James. In fact, in Nigel I think James sees something of himself.'

'What time are we likely to dock tomorrow?' Stella asked, feeling that she ought to change the subject, although she would have loved to have probed more deeply. 'I seem to have slept a lot since we came aboard.'

'Some time after breakfast. Hopefully not too early though!'

54

After breakfast the next morning, they were nearing their destination and went on deck to have a look. Thomas and the children were there and Janet hurried back to the cabin for her camera to take pictures of the children.

She promised to write and send them a photograph and they all managed a beaming smile of thanks. Nevertheless they looked a little forlorn as they stood with their few possessions while Thomas saw Janet and Stella into a rather battered-looking taxi.

Janet was eager to get her photographs to the laboratory immediately, so while they checked their luggage into their hotel, she asked their taxi to wait for them outside, afraid that they wouldn't get another one for a while.

On this occasion, Janet wasted no time and they were soon back in the taxi and being driven to the laboratories which were not far away. Stella paid the taxi driver, and the two of them stepped out onto the pavement.

'Remember not to tell them that they're anything special,' Janet urged. 'It's important that no-one knows what they are. Just say we need a high quality job because they're to be printed in a magazine later.'

The white-coated technician in the lab assured Stella of the excellent standard of their workmanship and that the prints and negatives would be ready for collection the following morning.

Their business concluded, Stella and Janet

wandered from the air-conditioned coolness of the laboratories into the scorching heat and noise outside.

'Let's go and have a coffee,' Janet suggested. 'I know a good place where I've been with James. And it has air-conditioning!'

'No wonder the heat is stifling—the hills must shelter the town from much of the breeze.' Stella remarked.

They entered a small cafe where Stella ordered coffee. The interior was cool and it was pleasant to sit and watch the colourful scene outside.

They took their time over their coffee and feeling refreshed, Stella agreed with Janet's suggestion that they could have a walk to the waterfront before returning to their hotel. There was a breeze coming from the sea and they spent a few minutes watching the colourful yachts in the bay.

They returned to their hotel by a different route, passing several clothes shops with attractive window displays. Stella drew Janet's attention to several things, but Janet showed little interest, her mind focused only on the object of their journey. After a while, Stella saw a hairdressing salon displaying pictures of hairstyles in their windows.

'Have you ever thought of a new look, Janet?' Stella ventured. 'I think you'd suit it.'

'I don't think any of these are really me,' Janet protested, looking with dismay at a picture of a smiling model with elaborate curls piled into a pyramid finished off by feathers and flowers.

'I didn't mean anything like that.' Stella laughed. 'What about something like this—it would only need regular trimming and would be no trouble at all. It would be nice to have a change.'

Janet looked doubtfully at the fair wispy fringe and the blonde hair falling to the shoulders of the model.

'It's not all that short—if you really wanted you could grow it again fairly quickly,' Stella persuaded.

'Not to the length it is now,' Janet retorted. 'And I'm too busy really to bother too much about my hair.'

'This style would be much easier to manage.'

'I'll think about it. I can't concentrate on hairstyles at the moment.'

Stella felt she could do no more but hoped the idea had been planted in Janet's mind and with a little help might take root. They soon reached the hotel and after a light lunch went upstairs to lie down. The room was pleasantly cool and Stella fell asleep almost immediately. She woke some time later to find Janet putting her book aside and wandering to the window.

When she woke up later, she found Janet was already showered and dressed for the evening.

'I hope I didn't disturb you,' Janet said. 'I can't think of anything but my pictures at present so I thought I would fill my time getting ready.'

'Well, if you give me a few minutes. I won't be long myself and then we can go out and sample the nightlife.'

The town was lively after dark with twinkling, coloured lights and music everywhere. They found an open-air restaurant overlooking the waterfront where delicious sea-food was served. They followed this with fresh fruit served in a locally-made liqueur.

Stella felt tired as they went back to the hotel—the liquor must have been quite strong. Janet, however, professed herself too anxious to sleep much. She could hardly bear to wait for morning when the prints could be collected.

The following day, they collected the prints and took them back to their hotel room where Janet spread out the prints.

'I never dared to hope that they'd be this good. Just look at them!'

Stella tried to display suitable enthusiasm, but the small creatures which so excited Janet looked very insignificant to her.

'I'll take them to the hotel safe,' Janet said, 'and then we'll go and enquire about a ship. I can't wait to show these to James.'

Stella had been looking forward to a few days' holiday and to her disappointment there was a ship in harbour which was to leave early the following morning and would be prepared to take them back.

'I'm sorry we'll be going so soon,' Janet apologised. 'But there's not much to see here—and the bathing is just as good on our island. Still we've got the rest of today. What would you like to do? We could go to the beach.'

'No. I think we should celebrate your achievement. Let's get our hair done and treat ourselves to a new dress each and have a really special meal on our last night here.'

'Do you really think I should?' Janet looked rather apprehensive.

'Yes,' Stella answered firmly as she led the way to the hairdressing salon she had noted the previous day.

'I expect you have to make an appointment,' Janet said, a note of hope in her voice.

'They don't look busy. We can go in and ask.'

Janet looked doubtfully at the style Stella had suggested.

'Are you sure this will look right on me?'

'It's fairly long. You often wear your hair in a ponytail, and if you decided you didn't like this, it would still be long enough to tie back.'

Stella hadn't intended to have her hair trimmed but it seemed the easiest way to get Janet inside. The salon was cool and shady—a relief from the brightness and heat outside.

After Stella explained what they wanted and the stylist set to work on Janet, she was delighted with the end result.

'I can't believe how different it looks. Thanks for persuading me, Stella.'

Stella was happy with Janet's new-found enthusiasm and once they'd finished in the hairdresser she helped her to choose an attractive jade green dress and darker green bag and sandals before they returned to their hotel to rest.

They enjoyed their celebration meal in the hotel before having a final walk round the town.

Janet was in a very contented mood and they made several small purchases and stopped for a drink before reluctantly deciding they ought to get back in view of their departure the following morning.

'I've really enjoyed this trip,' Janet said as they prepared for bed, 'but I'm looking forward to getting these prints back to the island.'

Stella had hoped the trip would last a bit longer. She wished there had been more time to think about the puzzling behaviour of the people on the expedition—and time to find out more about Adam from Janet.

There were some very odd situations involving him and Sir James, and there was also the possibility that Adam was involved with Charity in some way. Then there was the puzzling business when her clothes had been thrown in the sea and the ring had disappeared and the frightening way in which it had been returned.

From the sound of Janet's even breathing, Stella knew she was fast asleep, no doubt dreaming of her triumphant return. She almost envied her. It was a long time before her own troubled thoughts allowed her to sleep and she felt exhausted when she had to get up early the following morning. She would really rather not be preparing to return to the island so soon.

CHAPTER SIX

As Janet had anticipated, her pictures were greeted with amazement and delight by the other members of the expedition. Her new hairstyle was also admired. Adam thanked Stella when he joined her on the patio where she was reading a book.

'Jan's come back a different person,' he said, 'and I know it's due to your good influence. I'm really grateful to you and I know she is too.'

'She was so euphoric when she saw those prints it was quite easy to get her to the hairdresser. The success seemed to give a real boost to her self-confidence.'

'And that can only be a good thing,' Adam said grimly. 'For too long James has blocked her promotion, and now he'll have to realise that other universities will be only too happy to have someone like her on their staff. I hope she realises she has real bargaining power and she must use it. If she does, he'll respect her—power is something he understands.'

Adam seated himself nearby and Stella closed the book, but her desire to talk alone with Adam was thwarted when Sir James joined them.

'Did you see anything of Thomas before you returned?' he asked Stella.

'No. We didn't see him again after we said goodbye at the harbour.'

'Janet should have made a point of tracking him down before she left,' Sir James said angrily. 'She should never have returned without him. The weather's perfect now. We could have been diving.'

'There's plenty of time left to do all you want to do here,' Adam protested. 'Thomas needed some spare engine parts and various other items. It was sensible to combine that business with escorting the children.'

'He's no right to leave us cooling our heels here while he has a holiday. We are paying him. Janet and I must get on with writing up our discovery for publication and we can't produce a final version here.

'Also, I've received a letter which suggests there's funding available for research on underwater equipment. The wealth to be found under the sea-bed is becoming increasingly apparent and industry is prepared to invest in promising research. Years ago, of course, there wasn't so much importance attached to the kind of work Stella's father and I were doing. And it would be some kind of tribute to him if I took up the present challenge and carried on his work. But if I am to do this, no time must be lost.'

'We could go and have a preliminary look at

the wreck's position,' Adam suggested. 'Size up the problems and then when Thomas returns we'll be ready to start. We can easily get a crew together and go tomorrow, conditions permitting. Shall I make arrangements?'

'Yes—all right,' Sir James agreed hesitantly.

Over the evening meal Adam and Sir James discussed plans for the following day's expedition. Adam had fixed up a crew and they were to make an early start.

'I've got some reading to do, so I'll turn in now. I'll see you all in the morning,' Sir James said, preparing to leave.

'You don't need me tomorrow, do you?' Nigel, who had joined them, demanded.

'I think we should all go.'

'Count me out. I'm not organising the dive and I've seen the wreck anyway, so it'll be nothing new for me.'

Nigel turned and strolled out and the atmosphere was suddenly tense. Sir James was obviously angry and Janet, who had followed Nigel into the room, looked uneasy and embarrassed. Adam's face was set stonily.

'You didn't tell me Nigel had already seen the wreck.'

'You didn't ask, my boy,' his uncle returned blandly. 'He saw it the same day I did. The sea was very calm and we used a small boat with an outboard motor to sail through the reef. It's nothing short of a miracle that we decided to

64

take to the small boat and go exactly where we did.

'I pin-pointed the spot on our charts and have spent a considerable time since then making enquiries and getting permissions. This is a really important find and Nigel observed absolute secrecy on my instructions.'

Sir James then got up and left the room. There was an uneasy silence.

'Coffee anyone?' Janet asked.

Stella accepted the offer but Adam declined and he, too, left. The two women drank their coffee in silence and eventually Janet suggested they went for a stroll.

'We won't go out of sight of the house,' she said. 'But I just want to get out of here for a few minutes.'

'It must be disappointing for your day to end like this,' Stella said, 'but I'm sure things will be better tomorrow and nothing can take away the success you have achieved.'

'The antagonism between Adam and his uncle goes back some years,' Janet said slowly. 'Maybe I shouldn't be telling you because I don't know the full facts. But as you're working with us, it may help you to understand and I know you will be discreet.'

'Of course I will.'

'It was when Adam was in his final year at the university. He fell in love with a girl in the first year—a blue-eyed blonde who looked as though butter wouldn't melt in her mouth. It wasn't long before she was having an affair with James. Everybody knew about it but Adam.

'He was working hard for his finals and thought she, too, was working to pass the first year exams. He found out what was happening just before finals and about the same time his mother became ill. Naturally he was shattered and didn't achieve the grade he should have.

'I was a researcher then and knew Adam was a very bright student. The result was that instead of staying on for a higher degree as he had hoped to do, he left and obtained his engineering qualification elsewhere.'

'I'm surprised that he ever spoke to his uncle again,' Stella said.

'His mother's illness made it difficult. He didn't want to upset her—she was very fond of her only brother—and I think with hindsight he accepted the girl was probably as much to blame as James particularly because she must have been known James was married at the time.'

'I had no idea he had been married.' Stella was amazed.

'It didn't last very long, especially when there are temptations with so many attractive girls around.'

'I can't see why a young student should want an affair with an older man—particularly one she knows to be married.'

'I think Penny thought James was serious.

He was, and still is, a handsome man and very good company. In addition, of course, he was quite well off while Adam was hard up. Probably she thought, too, that as James would be marking her first year work, she was on to a good thing.'

'What happened to her?'

'James quickly lost interest, she failed her exams and left. James made it clear that he hadn't pursued the girl—she'd been more than willing, and I think even Adam eventually realised that his loss wasn't as great as he had thought at the time. Admittedly, it affected his career plan but as things have turned out he's doing very well and is highly respected in his field.'

'But even so, it seems surprising that he is willing to help his uncle,' Stella said.

'Unfortunately since around the time of his finals, Adam's mother has been dogged by illness. I know Adam has been employing a nurse so that she could continue living at home and that's been expensive. Time is not on her side, and James offered to stand the cost of the treatment if Adam would help him here.'

'I'm glad you told me, Janet. It makes things a lot easier to understand. There's bound to be quite a bit of tension between them.'

Both women were wrapped in their own thoughts as they made their way back to the house. All was quiet and peaceful and Stella was glad that at last she had learned the cause of the trouble between uncle and nephew.

How could he pretend he had loved only Stella's mother when in fact he had been married and apparently had a string of relationships? She seriously doubted that the ring he had given her had ever been intended for her mother. She thought it was probably the price he was prepared to pay to get hold of her father's research work, and that he would have been willing to have an affair with her in order to achieve this end if he had received any encouragement.

*   *   *

The following morning, as arranged, they set sail early. Nigel was nowhere to be seen. Sir James and Adam seemed to be on amicable terms as they talked with the crew while Janet and Stella chatted together.

Adam switched on the radio to listen for reports of any adverse weather conditions. Their progress was slow as they carefully negotiated shallow passages through the reef. Eventually they dropped anchor and went below for refreshments. A cooling fan provided a welcome breeze.

Afterwards Stella and Janet cleared away and stayed in the cabin listening to the radio as the boat was set in motion. Eventually they realised it was circling and the engine shut off. Then they heard James's voice.

'I think it's shifted a bit, but it's still there!'

Janet and Stella rushed on to the deck. Stella didn't know what to expect as she joined the others at the rail. At first she could see nothing, then a grey shape became visible far below.

'That's no ancient wreck—that's a submarine!' Adam gasped.

'Precisely, my boy. A U-boat. I always suspected it could lie in this area but it's a miracle that I actually found it.'

'We can't enter that. Surely it will have the status of a war grave.'

'It went down after the war. I've been in touch with governments and have permission to go in. There are special reasons . . . I'll explain later. I have a plan and know precisely the area we need to enter. Can you do the job?'

They circled slowly, stopping at frequent intervals to survey the submerged vessel from several angles and take soundings.

'It can be done,' said Adam slowly, 'so long as conditions are ideal and provided it doesn't move nearer the edge of the shelf, but I'm not happy about it. I'll need to discuss it with Thomas. He's more familiar with conditions here than I am.'

Sir James drew Adam aside and spoke in low tones. He then gave orders for the return journey and the crew obeyed with alacrity, seeming happy to be leaving the area. Janet and Stella returned below to get away from the strong sunshine.

'There'll be no time to drop anchor on the way back,' Janet said, 'otherwise we shan't arrive before dark and there are no lights on the jetty. We'll keep the crew supplied with drinks and fruit—they need plenty of liquid in these conditions.'

'How will they manage when the actual diving takes place? Surely that will take quite a lot of time?'

'We'll stay on an island where we have built temporary shelters. They're a bit primitive but as it's so warm here, we can manage. They'll probably need to spend a few days diving, maybe longer if conditions aren't perfect.'

The return journey was uneventful and they reached the villa as dusk fell. When Stella went in for the evening meal, Adam and his uncle were arguing while Nigel listened, a sardonic grin on his face.

'I'd a right to know the whole truth,' Adam snapped.

'As far as you're concerned the age of the vessel makes no difference. You are employed by me as a diver, operating the most modern equipment available. The organisation and the responsibility for our actions are mine. I wanted the most able person I could find for the job and I have complete confidence in your ability.'

'But what can there possibly be in that sub

70

that's worth the risk? Do you really have authority to break into a German U-boat? Who is in a position to give you the go-ahead?'

'I have spent considerable time and money checking out this particular vessel,' Sir James replied. 'When we first found it we managed to get an identification mark. Naturally in the normal course of things you wouldn't expect to find such a vessel in this area, but a few disappeared after the war when they were carrying looted treasure to South America.

'This particular vessel was carrying top scientists and their secrets. They never reached their destination but on board are particulars of discoveries which many governments would do anything to possess. Such things are safer in our hands.'

'It might be better if they remained at the bottom of the sea,' Adam remarked. 'And after all this time under water, any documents will probably be seriously damaged and useless.'

'Naturally, I checked everything out. They were very carefully packaged and sealed so that if necessary they could be thrown overboard and still survive. With hindsight I realise I was wrong not to confide in you earlier, but I can only apologise for that. If the sub had disappeared, as seemed possible, explanations would have been unnecessary.'

'I think you will have to explain the situation to Thomas,' Adam said. 'He will be reluctant to work in that area even on an ancient wreck,

71

so there is no point in risking a disruption when we get there. You will have to convince him of the need to get into the wreck.'

'He'll be OK if you offer enough incentive,' Nigel sneered. 'You'll have to bribe the man.'

'That's enough,' Adam snapped. 'You think money can buy anything—and you're wrong.'

'In this case, Nigel's quite right,' Sir James interrupted. 'When it comes to dealing with the people here, he knows best.'

With a smirk, Nigel turned away and asked Stella about the trip. Janet joined them and monopolised the conversation until the meal was over. Afterwards Sir James produced plans he had obtained of the submarine and her cargo. He suggested the others take them away and study them.

'I haven't seen the sub's latest position, so I wouldn't be much use,' Nigel grinned. 'I'll relax in the garden with my fiancée instead. What would you like to drink, Stella?'

'I need Stella to do some urgent work for me,' Sir James said sharply. 'We can't waste time. Hopefully Thomas will come back on the mailboat, then we can get on with our task and by then my letters will be ready for despatch.'

'We could spread these plans out better in the office, Jan,' Adam suggested. She agreed and the two went out carrying the plans with them.

'I'll take a bottle to my room and drown my sorrows,' Nigel said. 'If you finish your work in the next hour or so Stella, give me a call and I'll have a nightcap with you.'

'You've done enough drinking.' Sir James said. 'Get yourself to bed. Divers need to be fit.'

Nigel muttered under his breath as he departed and Sir James gave an exasperated sigh.

'The trouble with that young man is his constant need to be occupied or entertained. He's not happy with the simple life here. If Thomas hadn't taken himself off, or Adam had been man enough to carry on without him, we'd have no problems.'

Stella didn't reply. She was tempted to remind him that originally he'd said Nigel was coming to do his own work and was helping Adam only because he would be around.

'What will you have to drink?' Sir James asked, putting on some music.

'Lime juice, please. But shouldn't we get on with the work first?' Her employer smiled.

'There isn't really any work to do. I just wanted us to have a talk. There's been little time until now, and as soon as we've cracked the problem of the sub I shall have to get back.'

He handed her a glass of lime juice and poured one for himself. He moved his chair closer to hers and drew a photograph from his pocket. 'Have you seen this before?'

Stella took the faded print from him and

73

studied it. The tall white-coated figure of Sir James was unmistakable. With surprise, she realised the other white-coated figure was her father—looking very much younger and slimmer, but with signs of the baldness which was to come already visible.

'No, I haven't seen this picture before.'

'The figure in the background is your mother.'

Stella gasped. Except for the old-fashioned hairstyle, it might have been a picture of herself.

'As I told you, my dear, you are very like your mother. I have several old pictures at home, but these are the ones I carry around. I have very fond memories of the old days— regrets, too! Your parents must have had pictures of our working life together—did they never show them to you?'

'No,' Stella replied, wondering if her parents preferred to forget their earlier relationship with Sir James. There had been some disagreement, she knew. And Adam had hinted that Sir James had spoiled her father's research chances.

'Let's go out on the terrace and get some air, my dear. It's such a lovely evening. If only we had these balmy breezes at home!'

He took their drinks and Stella followed. The huge moon illuminated the garden and the breeze from the sea gently rustled the leaves.

'There's something special about this island. Even its name can loosely be translated as "Island of Love". If I could re-live my life, I would behave differently. But sadly now it is too late . . .' Sir James gazed out into the distance, his voice tailing off into not much more than a whisper.

'I'll get some more juice,' he said, rising to his feet. 'The heat makes one so thirsty.' He returned with replenished glasses and sat down again purposefully.

'As I mentioned earlier, my reasons for returning to England quickly are two-fold. First there is Janet's discovery and secondly there is now research funding available for the type of equipment your father was working on. I would be honoured to be able to continue his work and I'm sure that is what he would have wanted.'

He paused then added, 'So I beg you, as soon as we return, to let me have all your father's notes and papers. Such things will, of course, be no use to you, and would be of value to no-one else, but I will examine them with care and may be able to build on some of his basic ideas. That way I will feel that his work has not been in vain.'

Stella hesitated. While she would be happy for her father's work to be carried on, she resented the devious way in which her employer was trying to get hold of it. She longed to talk the matter over with Adam, whose judgement she felt she could rely on. But Sir James was waiting for her answer.

'I'll think about it when we get home and I can sort things out.' She smiled, hoping the non-committal reply would satisfy him. And with relief she saw Adam coming towards them.

'You have made me a very happy man, my dear,' Sir James retorted as with a theatrical gesture he raised her hand to his lips. 'Ah, Adam, my boy,' he said. 'Come and have a celebration drink. We have just reached an understanding. I hope there will be cause for congratulation after we get back to England.'

Adam's face gave nothing away as he looked at them.

'You are constantly to be congratulated on your various successes, uncle,' he said lightly. 'I came to tell you Janet will be along in a minute. We have some champagne and I think we should toast her recent success.'

'An excellent idea. We don't want an old and valued colleague to feel left out of things.'

'I'm sure she won't feel left out. Her discovery more than justifies the expenditure on this trip. She has made scientific history and will no doubt get some exciting offers to lead her own research team. Can't you see the change in her already?'

'What do you mean?' his uncle asked uneasily, but Adam was prevented from replying because Janet appeared. She was wearing the new dress and walked with a new assurance and confidence.

'Janet, my dear,' Sir James said as he rose to greet her, 'we must drink a toast to your recent success and to the future success of all our projects.'

'Come on, Stella,' Adam said. 'We'll get the champagne.'

Stella rose and followed him from the room. He didn't speak until they reached the kitchen. Then he turned to her, a look of anger on his face.

'Can't you see what's happening? James is only amusing himself with you. I've seen it all before. There's no way he'll ever marry you. I don't know what Jan sees in him and I wish she'd come to her senses. But please try to understand what his philandering does to her. Just keep away from him!'

Stella was furious at his accusation.

'It's not easy to avoid someone who is employing you,' she replied. 'But I don't want your uncle. He's my employer for goodness sake.'

'I'm sorry, I shouldn't have jumped to conclusions.' Adam focused on the ground. 'I expect James was trying to rile me.'

'Which doesn't seem difficult,' she remarked sarcastically. 'We'd better return with this champagne before it gets warm.' She picked up the tray of glasses and heard Adam following her. Janet had brought Nigel to join

77

in the celebration, someone had put some lively music on and as the cork popped, the atmosphere seemed suddenly lighter.

Sir James was once again in a happy mood and as he talked, Stella found herself laughing at his stories, in spite of herself. Time passed quickly and she was surprised to see how late it was when Sir James finally said he should go to bed.

Since their exchange in the kitchen, Stella had tried to avoid Adam, and as Nigel was constantly at her side it hadn't been too difficult.

'Let's go swimming early tomorrow,' Nigel suggested. Stella agreed, and for a moment thought Adam was going to suggest joining them. However, after a momentary hesitation he turned away and followed Sir James and Janet.

'Now we've got rid of them, how about another drink, Stella?'

'No thanks. If we're going swimming early tomorrow, we'd better get some sleep.'

'I suppose you're right. I should keep fit for all this diving we're going to do. I look forward to tomorrow morning then.'

CHAPTER SEVEN

The following morning, Nigel and Stella went for their swim. There was no sign of anyone else. Nigel was a very strong swimmer and Stella admired his prowess.

'Come on, Stella,' he called as he swam out to sea.

'No—I'm staying here—I can't swim like you,' she shouted back.

'You don't have to worry. I'll look after you,' he called, but she ignored his request to join him. After an hour or so, the sun grew stronger and Stella decided it was time to go back. Reluctantly Nigel agreed.

'I've really enjoyed this morning,' he said. 'I need company—pleasant company. We must do this again. Unless my time is fully occupied here, I get very bored. I much prefer civilisation. There won't be anything to do when we get back, so I'll challenge you to a game on the computer.'

'All right—so long as there is no work for me to do.'

After a leisurely shower, Stella joined Nigel in the lounge. Janet was there already. She told them Thomas was back and the equipment was being checked and assembled so that diving could start during the next few days, conditions permitting.

'Are you coming to help?' she asked Nigel.

'No. The arrangements are in Adam's capable hands. I agreed to help with the actual diving and until that starts I'm keeping out of things. Stella and I are going to play computer games. Do you want to join us?'

'No thanks,' Janet replied shortly, as she hurried off.

'I'd have got a shock if she'd agreed to play with us,' Nigel laughed. 'I only asked her because I knew there was no chance. She'll be hanging around James, and there's no way she'll succeed with him, despite the new image. Although I must admit she looks almost attractive now. But come on—let's get out of here before someone else tries to press-gang us.'

Soon it was time for the light lunch they usually enjoyed before the afternoon siesta. Stella was totally unprepared for the scene which greeted them when they reached the dining area. Sir James and Thomas were facing one another across the table. Both were shouting and gesticulating. Adam and Janet, were trying to pour oil on the troubled waters.

The raised voices stopped as Stella and Nigel entered, but the atmosphere was tense. The silence was broken by Thomas.

'I will go before there is blood on my hands. You will get no more help from me—or from my people.'

He turned and strode off, leaving an awkward silence behind him.

'You are quite incredible!' Sir James snapped, turning on Nigel, who looked very shamefaced.

'What on earth can we do now?' Janet demanded, almost in tears.

'What's up?' Nigel asked.

'You know perfectly well,' Sir James told him. 'Why the hell can't you leave their girls alone. You know it only causes trouble.'

'I've only acted in a friendly way,' Nigel retorted defensively. 'I get so bored around here.'

'You have been warned before. You know their code of conduct is different from ours. When we're here, we must abide by their customs.'

'I did no harm . . . I reckon Charity found out and caused trouble.'

'Whatever happened, you've finished off our work here. I suggest you disappear for the rest of the day while we talk things over. If you value your life, don't leave the house.'

Without another word, Nigel turned on his heel and went out. Stella hesitated, wondering if she should leave as well. Noticing her uncertainty Sir James asked her to stay.

'I think Thomas is big-headed and presumptuous,' Sir James said eventually. 'After all he doesn't own the island or its people. Is there anything to stop us from carrying on without him and his crew?'

'They own the boat,' Adam reminded him. 'We hire it from them when we are here.'

'And we have hired it for our visit, so technically it's still ours.'

'But we've hired both the boat and crew,' Adam objected. 'It may not be possible to split them. We couldn't manage everything ourselves and I'm sure no-one else has Thomas's knowledge of these waters.'

'He's just a bullying, jumped-up nobody,' Sir James snapped. 'A bit of power has gone to his head. He threatened us with violence!'

'In the circumstances he could hardly be blamed,' Adam said.

'It's a pity you hadn't managed to spend more time with him,' Sir James replied. 'And if Stella hadn't gone off with Janet . . .'

'Uncle, there was no reason for any of us to have acted as nursemaids. You told me that Nigel was coming to do his own work—but I've seen no evidence of it. What's done can't be changed now, and it's no use having an inquest.'

'So you think we should just pack up and go home and tell other departments at the university that work here is ended because one bullying native threatens us.'

'I didn't say that.'

'What alternative have we got then?'

Adam didn't answer immediately and his

uncle added impatiently, 'I'm furious at Nigel's stupidity, but at least he's got some guts. If he'd been organising things we'd have been getting on with the job long since.'

'That's not fair,' Janet snapped. 'There's no point taking out your frustration on other people. That won't help.'

Stella was surprised to hear Janet attack Sir James. At last Adam spoke.

'Let's have lunch and a rest. Then when it's a bit cooler, I'll go and see Thomas and talk things over. We may be able to come to some agreement.'

Nigel refused an invitation to have lunch in the dining-room and Janet took him a tray. The atmosphere was gloomy. No-one wanted to eat much, or to talk, and Stella was glad when she could retire to her room.

The morning swim must have tired her because she managed to sleep soundly and it was late when she awoke. Sir James and Janet were in the lounge. She learned that Adam had departed on his peace mission some time ago and had not yet returned.

'That murderous Thomas has probably killed him,' Sir James muttered.

'Don't be ridiculous,' Janet replied. 'They have always got on well together and Thomas will no doubt have calmed down by now.'

Despite Janet's confidence, Stella was very worried, and found herself uttering silent prayers for his safe return. It was a tremendous relief to her when he arrived some time later, looking hot and tired.

'How did you get on?' Janet demanded eagerly.

'He and his crew will help us as originally agreed after Nigel has left the island and agreed to never come back.'

'Thank goodness for that,' Janet said with relief.

'You shouldn't have given in,' Sir James protested. 'Why should Thomas think he can dictate to us who shall be included in our expeditions? Has he no gratitude for all we've done here?'

'James, stop being so difficult,' Janet declared firmly. 'And you know as well as I do that Nigel doesn't fit in here. He works well in his own environment, but he lacks stability. I will be happy to see the back of him.'

'I assume that Adam will side with you and I'm defeated then. How do you feel about Nigel leaving, Stella? You and he seemed to get on well.'

Stella was surprised at his question and didn't know what to say.

'Come on, I want your opinion. Would you like Nigel to go or stay?'

'I can't express an opinion when I don't know what happened, but if Nigel has knowingly caused offence to the people of this island, it seems to me quite reasonable that he should be asked to leave.'

'That settles it then. I'll go and tell him to pack.'

'The ship leaves tomorrow morning,' Adam said.

Smiling, Sir James went out. It was amazing how quickly his anger and indignation could fade. Stella had a feeling that now she had been made to feel some responsibility for Nigel's departure, he was happier.

'Dinner's going to be a happy affair—worse than lunch,' Janet said uneasily. 'I'll be glad when Nigel's gone. It doesn't make things any easier when James and I are going to have to work with him when we get back. I wonder if we could make this a sort of farewell dinner and try to ignore the reason for his leaving.'

'He'll be glad to get away. He can't stand the place for long. I don't know why he came,' Adam said.

'It was James's idea . . .' Janet stopped abruptly, realising she was saying the wrong thing. 'I'll go and see if I can talk them into the idea of the farewell dinner,' she added, as she hurried out.

'I thought James was responsible for the addition to our party,' Adam said bitterly. 'I shall be relieved when this job is finished.'

The atmosphere at dinner proved to be less strained than Stella had expected. The scientists seemed to have resolved their differences, or at any rate were putting a good face on things, and no reference was made to the cause of Nigel's early departure. Nigel himself was quieter than usual, though by no means downcast.

After the meal he asked Stella to accompany him into the garden. As it was his last night she didn't like to refuse. They took their drinks on to the patio. It was pleasant in the moonlight, with the soft warm breeze and the distant murmur of the sea.

'I've been an utter fool,' Nigel said, dropping the cheerful facade he had displayed during the meal. 'James tore a strip off me. And he was right. I lack stability. It affects my behaviour and my work. It's time I turned over a new leaf. I wish I could stay here now.

'Strange, isn't it? I thought I couldn't wait to get back home. But now I long to stay—I want to be with you. Until today I hadn't realised how very much you mean to me. I love you dearly, Stella. But there's no way I can stay here with you now. So will you come away with me tomorrow?

'From now on I am going to be a very different person. I need you. And the others can manage without us. Please come with me, Stella.'

She was amazed—she hadn't expected this!

'No—I'm sorry, very sorry—but that's impossible . . .'

'Is there someone else?'

She hesitated slightly before answering 'yes'. Although she knew how she felt about Adam, she wasn't entirely sure he felt the same way.

'I hope it's not James.'

She hesitated again, not wanting him to probe further, yet reluctant to tell him to mind his own business.

'No, of course it's not James,' she said firmly, hoping he would realise it was a subject she had no wish to discuss.

'I don't want to interfere,' he said gently. 'But don't ever trust James. His love in life is himself and from what I can gather, he will do almost anything to get his hands on your father's work. I know he has hinted about his affection for you, but believe me, he is incapable of loving anyone.

'Remember I'm your friend, and however stupidly I've behaved, I'd be willing to look at any papers you might have and give you an honest opinion. If you never have any deeper feeling for me, I'd like to think we are friends. I've been happy while I've been with you. You've enjoyed my company, haven't you?'

'Yes, you know I have.'

'Then promise you'll get in touch with me when you return,' he urged. 'If it's only friendship you want, I won't press for anything else.'

He seemed so unhappy that she hadn't the heart to refuse. And when she suggested it was time they went inside, he kissed her gently before they did. In some ways Stella was sorry to see him go. She felt that she now understood him better and he had been enjoyable company when the cheerful side of his nature had been to the fore.

On the other hand she thought, after Nigel had gone, Adam might be more relaxed and friendly. So it was with a lighter heart that she went to her room and removed the ring, thankful that now there was no longer any need to keep up the pretence of her engagement to Nigel.

CHAPTER EIGHT

The following day after Adam had taken Nigel to the harbour and seen him aboard, preparations for the dive forged ahead. He brought Thomas back and they entered into long discussions. Stella thought it wise to keep out of the way and was pleased when she was asked to accompany Janet to collect supplies of food for the expedition.

'We don't know how long it will take,' Janet explained. 'And while the work is going on we will stay on a small uninhabited island where we've set up some huts—a bit primitive, but great fun.

'It's just within the reef and protected to some extent, so if conditions aren't good in the area we're working, we can wait there until things improve.'

Janet drove the van competently and it seemed to Stella a much smoother journey than she usually experienced on the rough island tracks.

Janet's list was a long one, and shopping a leisurely process. Everywhere they went, there were friendly greetings and invitations to stay a while, so their task took a long time.

'It's very touching,' Janet said as they

stowed away their purchases and set off, leaving behind a beaming, waving shopkeeper and his wife and large family, 'these people are really poor and yet so hospitable and willing to welcome any stranger who calls. It makes me ashamed sometimes. Life here will change eventually—in some ways it needs to—but it's sad that with the eventual coming of modern equipment and consumer goods, no doubt greed and selfishness will come too.'

The sun was becoming very hot as they returned with the heavily-laden van.

'We'll have a meal and a rest and then take this lot straight to the boat,' Janet suggested. 'There's no point in unpacking any of it.'

'We're taking a tremendous amount of food,' Stella said.

'We may not need all of it,' Janet replied, 'but where we're going there are no means of replenishing our supplies. We may get fresh fish and coconuts, and we have planted a few things which might have survived but we need to take too much rather than too little.'

'I feel a bit awkward about going on this expedition where I'll have to face Thomas,' Stella confessed. 'After all the problems with Nigel and the fact that we were supposed to be engaged . . . Thomas did warn me about Nigel's weakness . . . it can't look good when it appears I've ditched the man I'm supposed to love because he's in trouble.'

'Don't worry,' Janet told her. 'I'll have a

word with Adam, and he'll smooth things out so there's no embarrassment. Thomas might well be upset that he's hurt you by throwing out your supposed fiancé. He's a very gentle character really.'

The remainder of the day was spent loading supplies and equipment and everyone was to have an early night in preparation for a dawn start the following morning. After the evening meal, Sir James discussed final plans with Janet and Adam. He apologised to Stella for neglecting her as they had a drink before retiring.

'I haven't felt neglected.' She smiled. 'I enjoy reading and swimming and my duties here haven't been taxing—it's been like a holiday.'

'Do you know much about astronomy?' he asked.

'Not really. At home I can just about pick out the major constellations.'

'Come outside and I'll show you the ones visible here.'

Obediently she followed him on to the terrace and listened as he pointed out various stars and explained their positions. The depth of his knowledge was amazing.

'Contemplating the heavens makes one realise how insignificant we really are,' he remarked. 'Yet some people are remembered long after they have departed this life . . . if you allow me access to your father's work, it may be that he could join that selected band.

'Nothing would give me greater happiness than to perform that service for my old friend. And meeting you has made me feel much closer to him.'

To Stella's relief, Adam and Janet joined them, and she was able to make her escape. She hoped that by the next morning Sir James would be too absorbed in his new project to press her any further on the subject of her father's papers.

While she would be happy to see the work carried on, she was becoming increasingly incensed with her employer's methods of trying to get hold of it. She resented his apparent belief that he just had to hint at a feeling of affection for her and she would agree to his request. How could a man of his intelligence be so insensitive? He must think her stupid, and that hurt most of all.

*   *   *

They set off very early in the morning. The larger vessel which they were now using had a cheerful crew who sang as they worked. Thomas and Adam conferred with Sir James as they checked equipment.

'Let's go below—it's getting rather hot,' Janet suggested. 'We'd better tune in for weather reports. Thomas reckons there's a storm coming—although so far there's been nothing about it on the radio.'

'Then he's probably wrong,' Stella said. 'Where did he get his information?'

'Sometimes, if you've lived on the islands for a long time, you get a feeling for that kind of thing.'

In the cabin, Janet switched on the radio and a cooling fan. Stella remarked on the speed at which they were moving.

'Yes—we should reach our destination much more quickly today. Of course they'll have to slow down as we negotiate a channel through the reef. It's much more difficult with a vessel this size.'

As she spoke, orders were shouted above and the ship began to move very slowly, turning frequently. From time to time, members of the crew came down to the galley and helped themselves to refreshments.

Janet and Stella did likewise and after a while they felt the vessel's speed increasing and Stella was aware of a pronounced lifting and sinking movement and realised that now they had left the sheltered waters of the reef. Everything on deck seemed much quieter.

'They've stopped singing now,' she remarked.

'Yes,' Janet said uneasily. 'The men don't like the area we're approaching. It's dangerous unless the sea is very calm. Fortunately for us they trust Thomas and if he decides at any point to call off the expedition for the day, we'll just have to go along with his decision.

That's our agreement.'

Despite the fan, the heat in the cabin was becoming oppressive. Stella felt a sense of foreboding and the atmosphere also seemed to affect the usually insensitive Janet.

'I'll be glad when this trip's over,' she muttered as the engines stilled and the ship dropped anchor.

They went on deck and Stella stayed in the background as the others discussed the situation of the sinister grey shape beneath the water. 'It's shifted slightly since we first saw it,' Adam said.

'Nonsense,' his uncle snapped. 'And the place we should enter is accessible on the surface which is uppermost. Our cutting gear is the latest and getting in should present no problem to someone with your experience. And according to my information and calculations, the lifting gear should take the weight quite easily. We might even complete the job today.'

'Uncle James—you know perfectly well there's no way we can work down there before we've made a thorough examination. Thomas and I will have a good look from here and then go down.'

The two men clambered over the side and got into a small dinghy with an outboard motor. They cruised round for a long time, studying the submarine from every angle. When they returned Adam looked worried.

'She's lying on the edge of the shelf,' he said. 'And Thomas thinks she's unstable.'

'You can't know that unless you've examined the thing in situ,' Sir James remarked impatiently. 'And you don't have to search the vessel. The plan shows the exact location of the things I want. The sea's calm. It shouldn't be a difficult job. I can't see the vessel shifting in these conditions.'

'We're going down to have a look,' Adam said.

Stella watched, fascinated, as Adam and Thomas unhurriedly tested their equipment, donned their cumbersome gear and disappeared over the side. Then, with the others, she moved to the rail and watched the two men moving around far below in the clear water, communicating by gesture as they made their examination.

An uneasy hush had fallen over the spectators. The sun blazed down, yet Stella shivered as she experienced its fierce heat and watched the two human figures below. They looked strangely vulnerable, out of their own element. So much danger lurked in the powerful sea and their very lives depended on frail man-made equipment which could fail . . .

Stella's heart pounded and her anxiety for their safety was almost unbearable. She knew now without a shadow of doubt that she loved Adam with every fibre of her being and wanted desperately to make him feel the same way about her!

'Don't worry—they're all right,' Janet said as the two figures moved closer together and began their ascent. 'Let's make some more coffee.'

Stella would have liked to wait until the two were safely aboard, but she followed Janet to the galley. It was some time before Sir James and the divers joined them, and clearly relations were strained. There was much technical discussion in which Janet joined.

Stella gathered that there were unexpectedly strong underwater currents and Thomas felt the wreck was shifting, although they had been unable to observe any actual movement. He suggested they abandon the operation and return the following morning when conditions might be more favourable and they would have the whole day in which to work.

'We've no time to waste,' Sir James insisted. 'Surely you can get on with the job now! Just try out the cutting gear on this area ...'

He pored over the plan once more while Thomas and Adam reiterated the dangers.

'We'll go and take a look ourselves,' Sir James announced suddenly. 'You'll come down, won't you, Janet?'

'No,' Adam and Thomas said together, drowning Janet's assent.

'I'm quite willing to go,' Janet persisted.

'No,' Thomas said emphatically. 'There is

evil down there.'

'Superstitious nonsense,' Sir James told him. 'I intend to take a look myself.'

'Uncle, at your age it would be unwise.'

'I'm quite capable of surfacing if I'm not happy. I'm as fit as either of you two, I've probably done it more times than both of you put together, and I've got more guts,' he said angrily as he went out, followed by the other two men.

'I suggest we stay here until they've sorted something out,' Janet muttered uneasily. 'Thomas isn't going to agree to my going down with James, and he can't go alone, so maybe all three will go—otherwise we'll have to call it a day and return tomorrow, weather permitting.'

'Is it very dangerous?' Stella asked.

'It can be. But experienced divers are sensible and cautious. They're always aware of what could happen. I worry a bit about James though. In the interests of science he can be reckless, and they are going down quite a depth, although it doesn't look deep from the surface with the water being so clear.

'Still, this time I agree with James that while conditions are ideal Adam should get on with the job. It seems to me he and Thomas are getting paranoid about the whole thing.'

The radio, which had been playing in the background, began to issue a weather bulletin.

'That's all we need,' Janet said, as the impersonal voice of the announcer forecast worsening weather and sea conditions. Her concern was echoed by Sir James who had returned in time to hear the announcement.

'A good job we've decided to get on with it immediately,' he said. 'All three of us are going down. Will you come on deck and keep an eye on things, Janet?'

'What about the weather forecast?' she asked.

'Say nothing about it. We've a few hours yet,' he said in a quiet voice as he left the cabin.

Stella was shocked.

'Don't you think Adam and Thomas should be told conditions are changing—so they know not to spend too long down there?' she asked Janet.

'If those two had heard the forecast they would have used it as an excuse to call diving off for today. James knows the score and if things change they can surface fairly quickly. We want to get this job finished as soon as possible and get back to writing up my findings—my work was the prime reason for our being here.'

Stella felt Janet's attitude towards the divers was callous. Surely Adam and Thomas should have been told of the changing conditions. As she followed Janet on to the deck she reflected that Janet and Sir James were very much alike. For them, no sacrifice was too great in the pursuit of knowledge. It was an attitude she found hard to understand.

As she watched the three making their preparations she longed to warn the younger men. Despite his height, Sir James looked very thin and frail beside the other men. Surely Janet should have tried to dissuade him! But he was ready first, impatient as always. Thomas looked uneasily into the cloudless sky. Stella thought he must sense her anxiety as he turned towards her and made a gesture she was sure was meant to be reassuring.

Again, everyone crowded to the side as the three figures submerged. The descent, with its frequent halts, seemed to take a long time, and Stella became aware of a fitful breeze and increased movement of the deck beneath her feet. Her anxiety seemed to be shared by the crew. Thomas was their trusted leader and now, without him, they were ill-at-ease.

Stella gazed intently at the three moving figures far below. The water seemed less clear than it had been and the divers were more difficult to discern against the dark shape of the hull.

'It's time they were surfacing,' Janet muttered eventually and Stella felt her heart thumping with anxiety. At last two figures started to ascend, then hover, as they seemingly waited for the third. Then they disappeared again and eventually three figures appeared form the now-murky depths.

'At last,' Janet breathed with a sigh of relief.

The ascent continued slowly. Two of the figures looked calm and controlled, but the third figure was gesticulating and seemed to be trying to grab hold of the other two.

'James, be careful,' Janet gasped, a shocked expression on her face. 'It looks like narcosis—he's hallucinating . . .'

Hardly daring to breathe, Stella fixed her gaze on the scene below. It was like a slow-motion replay. Horrified, she watched as Sir James seemed to be trying to wrench at the tube attached to Adam's head gear. He was going to cut off the air supply!

'No!' she shouted in horror.

But the bulky figure of the third man eased Sir James away, while encouraging him slowly upwards. For a time the ascent progressed without incident then, as they neared the surface, the older man began to struggle again and the others seemed to be trying to calm him, while at the same time evading his outstretched arms. Stella felt overwhelming relief as Adam surfaced first and the crew prepared to help the divers aboard.

Briefly she closed her aching eyes and breathed a prayer of thankfulness. Janet's anguished shout made her look once again towards the divers. Still under water, Sir James was pulling at his own breathing apparatus and struggling frantically.

Thomas managed to get him to the surface and suddenly Adam was supporting the now-

100

still figure while Thomas and the crew struggled to heave it from the water.

'Get my black bag from below, Stella,' Janet gasped. 'Next to the first aid kit. Quick!'

Stella flew below, grabbed the bag and hurried back. Thomas was holding Sir James as though he were a rag doll. Then he lowered him to the deck and Janet took over, pressing vigorously on the still figure, her mouth to his while Adam knelt beside them holding his uncle's wrist, an anxious expression on his face.

The sun had disappeared and the sky was a strange colour. The vessel creaked and a fitful breeze moaned. In the background, Thomas could be heard giving instructions to the crew.

'Open the bag,' Janet ordered and Stella held it open as Janet filled a syringe and plunged it into the limp figure.

'Thank God,' Janet whispered as Sir James breathed noisily and briefly opened his eyes. Adam brushed the wet hair from his forehead and glanced up at the glowering sky.

'Can we move now?' Thomas demanded.

'Yes,' Adam replied. 'I suppose we can't ride the storm out here?'

'No—impossible. Unless of course, we don't make it through the reef, then there's nothing else we can do.'

Large drops of rain were beginning to fall and there was a distant rumble of thunder. The crew obeyed Thomas's orders with alacrity and began to sing as they went about their tasks. Stella was sent below to arrange a bed for the invalid. As she reached the companionway, the vessel lurched and she would have fallen had Adam not caught her in his strong arms.

'Keep hanging on to something sweetheart,' he urged. 'There'll be a lot of movement soon but don't worry. We'll be OK.'

She went below, clinging to the rail. There was now a great deal of movement. It seemed as though the vessel was about to keel over as the mounting sea slapped against the portholes. It was incredible how quickly the storm had risen.

She seized cushions and made a bed for the sick man, collecting blankets which she had found near the first aid box. Despite her fear and anxiety, she couldn't forget the strength of Adam's arms and the tender way he had spoken to her.

Thomas and Adam carried Sir James down and the girls settled him on the cushions, dried him gently and covered him with the blankets. He was shivering but conscious. Stella made him a warm drink while Thomas padded away, his feet still bare and water running in rivulets down his dark skin. Adam was already wearing sandals, shirt and shorts which clung damply to his wet body.

Janet held a drink to Sir James's lips and he gave her a wan smile.

'I'm sorry I've been a trouble to you all,' he gasped.

'Don't talk. Just rest till you feel stronger,' Janet said gently.

The vessel was moving more quickly now and the buffeting waves and strong wind made conversation difficult. Adam drew Stella towards the galley.

'We'll have a drink ourselves,' he said, bending close so that she could hear him above the storm, 'and then I'll try and persuade Thomas to let me take over soon. He saved James's life—or rather a combination of his strength and Janet's medical skill.'

Despite her fear as the storm increased its fury, Stella thrilled at Adam's nearness in the tiny galley and the frequency with which she found herself in his arms as they struggled to keep upright.

'Don't worry, darling. This old tub's very strong—and once we make it through the reef things will be better. Thomas knows the reef. I must go and take over now so that he can have a break.'

Stella was reluctant to let him go, but the warmth of his kiss and his promise to return soon comforted her. A few seconds later the huge figure of Thomas appeared. He now wore shorts but was still barefoot.

Despite the danger, his beaming smile was undiminished. Finishing his drink quickly, he thanked her, adding, 'I will return to the wheel and leave you two alone. He's a good man. Hold on to him.'

Once again, Stella realised that Thomas knew how she felt about Adam, but did Adam now feel the same way about her? She longed for his return, but he didn't come. The boat slowed and there was a lot of shouting and noise—banging and scraping—and the vessel stopped.

Stella froze. Had it been holed? If they had to abandon ship they stood no chance in the boiling, heaving water. 'Adam, please come back,' she begged silently.

After what seemed an eternity they were moving again, edging forward and stopping, and she suspected they were negotiating a passage through the reef. The wind seemed less strong and the noise, too, had abated and as the ship picked up speed once more there was less heaving. She could hear the men on deck singing again.

It now seemed that the danger had passed. at least temporarily. Would Adam remember his promise to return? She was reluctant to join Sir James and Janet. She wanted to be alone with him. She was contemplating going on deck herself when Adam re-appeared.

'Sorry to have been so long, but when we were coming through the reef just now, all hands were needed.'

'Is everything all right?'

'Yes. We had a few bumps, but no serious

damage. We're making for the small island we sometimes use as a base. Everything's under control now and we should be there before dark. I suppose we ought to go and check on the invalid.'

There was still a good deal of rolling and Adam held Stella firmly as they moved into the cabin. Sir James was propped up on cushions and wedged into a corner while Janet sat beside him to prevent him falling as the vessel rolled. He was looking more composed now.

'I must thank you for rescuing me,' the older man said hoarsely.

'I did nothing. Thomas and Janet did the real work. How do you feel?'

'Glad to be here. I suppose I now have to admit I'm getting too old.'

'Nonsense. You just need to approach things more calmly. You'll be fine when you've had a rest,' Janet said.

'You're all taking good care of me.' He smiled, and closed his eyes.

He looked very old and tired and Stella saw Janet's fingers close gently on his wrist. Noticing Adam's questioning glance she mouthed, 'He'll be OK.'

'We'll be arriving soon,' Adam said. 'We'll be on the sheltered side, so landing should be no problem. You'd better stay here while we get the huts ready. Do you want James ashore, or would you rather he stayed on board?'

'He'll be better on shore,' Janet said

decisively.

'Right then—we'll let you know when everything's ready.'

The vessel began to lurch again and Stella was thankful that Adam was still holding her.

'You haven't got your sea-legs yet,' he joked as she clung to him. 'We're turning to go round the island. Come and have a look. It's easier to keep your feet when you can see the waves coming.'

'It's stopped raining,' Stella said in surprise as she looked into the clear sky and felt the heat of the sun. Already the deck was dry and the sodden ropes steaming, although the wind was still strong. As they circled the small palm-fringed island the deck seemed more stable and the crew greeted the sight of the wooden jetty with cheers.

'That makes things easier,' Adam said with relief. 'We thought it might have collapsed.'

They tied up the vessel and the jetty was tested and found to be safe. Adam helped Stella from the boat. It felt strange to stand once more on a surface which wasn't moving. She moved hesitantly on her stiff and aching legs.

'You've tensed up as the boat rocked,' he explained. 'The stiffness will soon wear off. Shall I carry you?'

'Certainly not,' she said vehemently, and he laughed as he put a steadying arm round her.

The group of wooden huts was near the

shore. They were circular and had palm-thatched roofs. Two members of the crew were already sweeping them out and dislodging the beetles which had settled there. Adam and Stella carried inflatable mattresses and other necessary items. Sir James was to occupy a central hut with Janet and Stella on one side of him and Adam on the other.

The sun was low in the sky when Adam and Thomas brought Sir James ashore. To Stella's surprise he was walking, albeit slowly and leaning heavily on his companions. Lamps had been lit in the huts and as dusk fell, a fire was made outside and a smell of cooking filled the air.

'You can't have fish any fresher than this.' Thomas laughed. 'Half an hour ago it was still in the sea.'

The crew arrived with food from the boat and gathered cheerfully round the fire. Janet took her food into the hut where the invalid was resting, but soon returned, saying he insisted that she join the party outside. After the crew had departed to spend the night on their vessel, Janet said she would be sitting up all night with Sir James.

'Is that necessary?' Adam asked.

'Yes. He's had a severe shock and although he seems fairly well now, there could be a relapse. He needs to be watched.'

'I'll stay with him. If there is any problem I can call you straight away,' Adam suggested.

'No thanks. It's something I feel I ought to do. I wouldn't sleep anyway, knowing what could happen . . .'

Eventually it was agreed that Janet should stay with the invalid for the next few hours and then Adam would take over.

'We need to stay here for another day, to give the crew a chance to do the repairs,' he said. 'We took quite a battering coming through the reef. And probably it will be better for my uncle to have another day in which to rest.'

'Yes,' Janet agreed, 'he needs to rest, although he seems to have come through remarkably well. I can hardly believe it. I'd better get back to him now. Good-night.'

'I'll be along later, Jan,' Adam replied.

Janet went, leaving him and Stella sitting by the dying embers of the fire drinking coffee.

'We'd better keep this going for a while,' Adam said as he went to collect more fuel.

The strength of the wind had lessened. It was now little more than a whisper in the surrounding trees and the crashing waves were only a distant murmur. Adam attended to the fire and returned to sit beside her.

'It's been a difficult trip. I expect your legs will feel a bit stiff tomorrow. There was an odd moment when I thought we might not make it.'

'You didn't show it,' Stella said.

'Of course not.' He smiled. 'But it's amazing the thoughts that go through your mind when

108

you think your last moments may be near.'

This conversation wasn't what Stella had expected, or hoped for. Was he trying to tell her that his show of affection had merely been because he knew they were in danger?

'What do you intend to do when this trip is over?' he asked suddenly.

'My original idea was to work for a time on one of the big liners. I studied languages and wanted to travel. But when my mother died I decided to stay with Dad for a while and got a job in the school. Now I'll have to look round and see what's available.'

'You won't return to your job at the school then?'

'No, I don't think so.'

For a short time he was quiet and thoughtful and she wondered what he was going to say. Would it be what she was hoping to hear? Eventually he broke the silence.

'I feel embarrassed about asking you, and tell me to mind my own business if you like, but I know you realise that my uncle's overtures towards you were purely an attempt to cash in on your father's research.

'I understand better than you how his mind works and I want to help you. So, forgive me for asking, but I wonder what your financial position is. Although it would be difficult, would it help if I could get someone to suggest a possible fee?

'I don't need the money,' Stella answered.

'If your uncle had been straightforward I would have willingly given him the papers. I know Dad wouldn't have wanted his hard work to be wasted. But I would like my father's contribution to be acknowledged in some way.'

'My uncle is a wealthy and successful man. He has no difficulty in obtaining financial backing for his research. I believe the project he has in mind will be commercially successful. It could fund a scholarship in your father's name—say for a science student from his old school.'

'Oh, yes. That would be a wonderful idea—the sort of thing Dad would appreciate.'

'Would you like me to put the idea to Uncle James? I'm pretty sure he'll agree.'

'Yes. I'd be grateful if you would.'

'I'll do that as soon as the opportunity arises. I think I'd better see how Janet's getting on and you've had a tiring day. I suggest you get some sleep, there'll be plenty to do tomorrow.'

He helped Stella to her feet and put a steadying arm round her.

'Goodnight, my dear,' he said gently as she went towards the hut she was to share with Janet.

While she was pleased to have found a possible solution to one problem, her heart was heavy because the affection Adam had displayed towards her when they were in danger now seemed to have vanished.

CHAPTER NINE

The following day there was much work to be done on the damaged vessel. Adam helped the crew with repairs while Stella worked in the cabin and the galley. She hoped there might be an opportunity to talk with Adam but whenever she encountered him there were always other people around.

Janet remained with Sir James and by evening all was ready for an early start the following morning. There was a festive atmosphere as the whole party gathered round the fire. Sir James, though weak, was well enough to join them.

After the crew had departed Janet suggested it was time Sir James retired.

'There's a long journey ahead of us tomorrow,' she reminded him.

'But there's no work for me to do, so I can rest,' he said. 'I will just be an observer. If the submarine is still there we'll have to consider the position.'

'It's gone. We saw it moving,' Adam said.

'It might not have disappeared completely,' his uncle protested.

'I think we should take the shortest route back and make arrangements to return home as soon as possible so that you can have medical checks,' Janet declared.

'Nonsense. There's nothing wrong with me. I know now that I took an unnecessary risk. I won't do that again. They say a drowning man's whole life passes before him and I can vouch for the fact that when you're in difficulties in the sea your mind is strangely active.'

Stella reflected ruefully that the danger had apparently influenced Adam too, resulting at the time in a display of affection. Now the danger had passed the feeling had evaporated. He clearly enjoyed her company but something was preventing him from pursuing the loving relationship which seemed to have been there during the storm.

Stella saw that Sir James and Janet were preparing to return to their huts. Adam said he would see the fire was safely extinguished. Janet had gone with Sir James to ensure anything he might need was to hand. At last Stella realised she and Adam were alone and she felt she must try to detain him for a while.

'Do you think we shall be going through the reef to look for the submarine tomorrow?' she asked.

'I don't know. I'll have a word with Thomas and we'll see what conditions are like. I'm sure it won't be there but if Uncle James sees for himself he will be satisfied. Otherwise, he'll be insisting on another expedition and I know

Janet wants to get him back home. Don't you like the idea of going back to the scene of the disaster?'

'No,' Stella admitted. 'I was terrified. I'm glad you were around.'

'I'll be there tomorrow, so don't worry. But if conditions aren't ideal we certainly won't go beyond the reef. This visit hasn't been easy for you, has it?'

'No,' Stella agreed. 'There were problems with Nigel. I got on quite well with him but I didn't like being part of a deception—and the ring your uncle gave me to wear was one he said he had once bought for my mother. But I wonder if he really did.'

'I doubt it. He can be careless with the truth and I don't think sentimentality is one of his characteristics. He has been married and had a succession of women. At one time I was afraid he was going to add you to the number.'

'There was no chance of that. I knew from the beginning he was interested only in Dad's papers. It would have made things much simpler if he'd been honest. Then there was the strange incident when we first arrived and my clothes were thrown into the sea and the wretched ring was returned through the broken window.

'I never wanted to swim alone after that and I always took care to close the shutters in my room as soon as the light started to fade. I can't help feeling that someone here doesn't like me.'

'Don't worry. It won't happen again. I suspected someone and my suspicions proved correct. However I gave my word at the time that I would not betray a confidence. It was Charity, and she was very upset afterwards. She begged me to say nothing but she's now agreed I can tell you because I assured her that you would understand.'

'But why did she do it?'

'Last time Nigel was here he became infatuated with her. At that time she intended to marry Thomas, but believing herself in love with Nigel, she separated from Thomas. Charity is a very talented girl, as well as being beautiful, and Nigel had filled her head with ideas about the opportunities she would have in his country.

'Maybe at the time his intentions were serious, but in the end he left without her. The breach with Thomas was healed but when she heard that Nigel had returned with another girl she was furious—as Thomas was. She came across your dress and bag on the sand. She picked them up, not realising who they belonged to. She saw you returning and ran off, still carrying them.

'Later, in anger, she threw your things to the edge of the water. The ring fell out and she picked it up, afraid it might get lost and wondering if this was the ring which had been promised to her. She heard voices and did not have time to replace it without being seen.'

'I'm beginning to understand,' Stella said.

'She knew it would be dishonest to keep the ring but didn't know how to return it without giving herself away. She is very sorry and when I told her how much the incident had upset you, she agreed that I could put your mind at rest.'

'In the circumstances it was a pity Nigel came on this expedition.'

'Yes—but people like him and my uncle never seem to realise the hurt they can cause other people. They just assumed the whole thing would have been forgotten.'

Adam seemed lost in thought for a few moments, then he looked at his watch.

'It's getting late and we'll have to have an early start in the morning so I guess we ought to be getting some sleep.'

He stretched out a hand to help Stella to her feet and as she stumbled, held her in his arms for a moment.

'Good-night Stella, my dear,' he whispered, a hint of sadness in his voice.

When Stella reached the hut, Janet was reading. But she soon put the book aside declaring that they ought to get some sleep as Sir James seemed insistent on making the longer journey the following day. Like Adam had done, she realised that whatever the state of his health he was determined to find out if the wreck was still visible.

'Do you think it will be there?' Stella asked.

'No. And in a way I hope it isn't or James will stay on here and I don't think that would be wise.'

Stella found that sleep didn't come easily but when it finally did, her dreams were of shipwrecks and seeing Adam struggling in the water just out of her reach.

*   *   *

It was a relief to wake the following morning and discover that the sea was calm. In order to save time it was decided to breakfast after they had set sail. Quickly the huts were cleared and they were on their way. The crew had already eaten and were singing cheerfully as Janet and Stella prepared food for themselves and Sir James.

'He's very quiet—I'm a bit worried about him,' Janet whispered.

'But you want him to rest as much as possible, don't you? Surely it's better for him to sit quietly than to be wandering around.'

'Yes and he insists he's feeling OK but I know he won't admit to feeling ill if there's a chance that he can stay and complete the job. I just wish this trip was over.'

Stella went on deck when she knew the vessel was manoeuvring through the reef. It took a long time and she was amazed that they had managed to come through relatively unscathed when the storm was at its height. Once they were in the open sea she realised that the men were no longer singing and Thomas's usual broad smile was missing.

'The crew were anxious to get back home,' Adam assured her, noticing her apprehension. 'There's been a storm and naturally their families will be worried. There's no danger now and I am pretty sure that the wreck will be inaccessible.'

It seemed to Stella that the vessel was rolling much more now they had left the shelter of the reef and she was thankful to have him by her side as the reached the place where disaster had almost overtaken them.

Janet and Sir James appeared as the noise of the engine ceased. He still looked frail but refused to be helped as he made his way to the side to look down into the clear depths. It was as though the wreck had never been there.

'Are you sure this is the place?' he demanded.

'Yes,' Adam assured him.

'It might have moved without going into deeper water. We must make a search while we are here.'

Thomas started up the engines and circled slowly as they gazed into the depths. But the submarine had vanished. At last Sir James accepted that the search was futile and his bitter disappointment showed as he and Janet went below once more and the vessel turned for home.

In sharp contrast to Sir James's attitude, the crew went about their tasks singing and Thomas joined in, a huge grin on his face.

'Thomas is glad to be on his way back,' Stella remarked. 'He didn't like the submarine at all.'

'I'm delighted we didn't manage to get into her,' Adam confessed. 'I was shocked when I realised the type of job I'd undertaken. I would never have agreed had I known the situation before I got here. I have my own ideas about the kind of information she carried.'

'But wouldn't it be out of date after all these years, or damaged by the sea?' Stella asked.

'According to my uncle, the material was protected in case it was necessary to conceal it in the sea at any time. I suspect the scientists involved were working on population control —mass medication—more sophisticated and certain than crude brutality. Such information is better in the depths of the sea.'

Stella remained on deck until they had negotiated a passage through the reef once more and then went below with Adam. To her surprise she found that Sir James had recovered from his disappointment and was already planning to go home at the earliest possible moment.

'There are quite a few jobs you could do for me after we have left, Adam,' he said. 'I'll make out a list. Although the main task has been eliminated because you didn't get down to it in time, I'm sure you'll be prepared to stay on and try to achieve something.'

'Of course, uncle. I took leave in order to work for you and I'm willing to carry on. And before you go, you'll have to let me know what equipment can be left behind and what I should bring back to the UK.'

Stella went to the galley to get drinks while the other three continued to discuss the work which might be carried out by Adam. She hoped that she, too, might be left with some duties on the island after Sir James and Janet had left, but her hopes were dashed when she returned to find that very subject under discussion.

'Of course Stella must return with us,' Sir James was saying. 'I feel responsible for the daughter of my old friend.'

'There are several jobs she could do here and Adam is staying on . . . It seems a pity that Stella has seen very little of the island . . . You would be happy to stay here a bit longer, wouldn't you?' Janet demanded, turning to Stella. But before she could reply Sir James snapped, 'I wish Stella to return with us.'

Stella thought she saw a look of disappointment on Adam's face but Sir James's breathing had quickened noticeably, and Janet shot a warning glance at the others as she murmured agreement. Adam returned

119

on deck without saying anything and Stella busied herself in the galley.

It seemed a long time before their own island was sighted but eventually Stella heard shouts from the crew and went on deck to watch as the vessel drew nearer. Adam joined her at the rail but said little and she realised that he looked very tired.

Eventually, when they tied up, he arranged for Janet to drive Sir James and Stella to the villa, saying he would pack the diving equipment in the second vehicle and follow on later.

A shower and a change of clothing had never been more welcome and after a light meal, Stella was only too ready to tumble into a real bed. Adam had still not appeared when darkness fell, but Janet explained how much would still have to be done before the vessel was left.

'If Nigel had still been here things would have been very different,' Sir James muttered.

Stella went to her room with a heavy heart. She was relieved to hear Adam return, but saddened by the knowledge that she had so little time left on the island.

The following day, Janet kept her busy. She learned that Adam had gone to help Thomas with the boat. Janet insisted that Sir James must rest and he grumbled like a discontented child while Janet, with Stella's assistance, frantically worked on the artefacts in the laboratory.

At the evening meal, Stella learned that the vessel which was to take them away from the island was likely to arrive in the next couple of days. 'Will the Reverend be on it?' Janet demanded.

'Yes,' Adam replied.

'In that case, I must get some things ready for him to take away,' Janet fretted. 'There's so little time.'

'Don't worry, Jan. I'll see to them after you've gone. Just let me know what's to go.'

'If Stella had been staying on, she could have helped,' Janet said. 'She's quite aware of what's required.'

'Adam's perfectly capable of managing without anyone's help,' Sir James snapped.

'Yes—I'll see to everything,' Adam said soothingly, adding, 'Thomas wondered if Stella could visit them tomorrow. Charity would like to show her the workshop and ask her advice about something. It seems a pity for her to leave without seeing a little more of the island.'

'That would be a good idea,' Janet said enthusiastically. 'You'd enjoy the trip out, wouldn't you, Stella?'

Stella quickly agreed that she would like to go and Sir James gave a grudging consent.

'But you'd better make sure you've packed your things before you go,' he said. 'Everything in this place is totally disorganised. We might

121

have to leave at any moment.'

The following morning, Stella dressed with special care, looking forward to the drive with Adam, determined to enjoy his company, even if it was to be for the last time. To her surprise Thomas arrived in a small vehicle which looked even more decrepit than the ones she had travelled in before.

'That vehicle is Thomas's pride and joy,' Adam whispered. 'He insisted on coming to call for us. They are very hospitable people. I believe Charity has something she's made for you.'

'For me?'

'Yes. They have a sort of dress-making factory by the side of the school. Charity runs it and they have quite a thriving small business exporting garments to the islands visited by tourists. I think that's why Charity would like your ideas. You will know what appeals to tourists while Janet, nice though she is, hasn't much idea of style.'

Thomas greeted them with his usual wide grin and they squashed into the long bench seat at the front of the vehicle.

'Hold tight to Stella.' Thomas laughed. 'The door might fly open.'

'You know perfectly well it won't,' Adam said as he obediently put his arm round her.

Despite its appearance the vehicle ran well and Stella expressed her surprise at its smooth performance.

'I doubt if there's a better mechanic than Thomas anywhere,' Adam said. 'And he looks after this car as though it's a member of his family.'

Both men pointed out things of interest as they travelled and Stella was conscious all the time of Adam's nearness, his strong arm round her and the faint smell of his aftershave. This journey, she reflected, would always remain in her memory as a brief time of perfect happiness.

There was a certain uneasiness in Charity's manner as she greeted him. To Stella's surprise, Thomas asked for Adam's help with some problem in another village and they went off together, promising to be back as quickly as they could. After they had gone Charity, a look of embarrassment on her face, apologised for what she had done when Stella arrived on the island.

'I've forgotten about it,' Stella assured her. 'When Adam explained, I could understand how you must have felt.'

'You should be happily married like Thomas and me. Nigel would not make a good husband. I know that now. And Adam knew it too. He's been unhappy all the time he's been here.'

Stella was puzzled by the turn the conversation was taking but her eagerness to hear more was frustrated as people began to emerge from the large hut outside which they were standing, anxious to greet the newcomer.

Charity took Stella inside where women of all ages and some boys and girls were chattering as they worked. Finished garments hung on a long rail and Stella was amazed by the delicate embroidery and beadwork on many of the dresses.

'I'll show you some wedding dresses,' Charity said, preparing to take Stella into another room.

'I'm making these to go with them,' a young boy piped up and Stella turned to admire beautiful coronets of pearly shells and artificial flowers. 'They are lovely,' she gasped. 'You have a wonderful talent.'

'Shouldn't you be spending more time in school catching up on your reading?' said Charity with mock severity.

'I'll read all the time when I'm in hospital,' the boy said, adding importantly, 'I'm going away with the Reverend when he leaves here. I'm going to hospital to have my leg made better.'

Stella noticed a pair of crutches leaning against the wall and the boy's deformed leg. After admiring his work again, Stella followed Charity into the next room.

'The Reverend visits the island at intervals,' Charity explained. 'Last time he brought an American doctor with him. This doctor says he can straighten the leg but there is no time to lose. He will not charge for the operation but

124

of course there are still a lot of other expenses.

'We have managed to get quite a large sum of money together and Janet is sending some things which the Reverend will sell for us. The doctor reckons one day the boy will be able to walk and run around like the others. Do you like these?' she asked, uncovering a rack of wedding dresses.

'They're absolutely beautiful.'

'Try this one on.'

Stella slipped into the soft, cotton dress. It had a tiered skirt and bell-like short sleeves. From the low neck a swirl of diamante and pearl flowers spread across the bodice and sparkled on the skirt. She stood before the mirror entranced, and knew this was the way she would like to look on her wedding day.

'Do you like it? It needs taking in a little at the waist,' Charity said, eyeing the garment critically.

'It's the loveliest dress I've ever seen,' Stella said with sincerity.

'It's a present for you,' Charity said.

'I couldn't take it. I'm not getting married.' Stella didn't want to hurt Charity or reject her generous gift, but to her surprise the other girl laughed.

'You love Adam, don't you?' she said.

Stella, feeling embarrassed, didn't know what to say.

'And he loves you,' Charity added. 'The Reverend is arriving soon and we haven't a wedding this time. You and Adam could get married here and have a celebration you'd never forget.'

'But Adam hasn't asked me to marry him,' Stella protested. 'In my country a girl has to wait until she's asked.'

'You are not in your country now. I hurt Thomas when I thought I loved Nigel. When it was over I knew how wrong I'd been. I told Thomas I was sorry. We were both unhappy and there was no sense in that. We got married and we were happy again.

'I think it's the same with you and Adam. He was hurt that he loved you and you were going to marry Nigel. We could see how he felt. Thomas and I have made a little plan and the rest will be up to you.'

Charity refused to say any more on the subject and took Stella to see the school and watch the small children in what seemed like a nursery unit outside the workshop. The day wore on and eventually the workers started to collect their children and leave. Only one plump baby remained, gurgling happily as he struggled to pull himself up into a standing position.

'Who does that baby belong to?' Stella asked.

'That's my little Tom,' Charity laughed as she picked the child up. 'And it's time for his feed and bath.'

'It'll be dark soon,' Stella remarked. 'I

thought Thomas and Adam weren't going to be long and they've been away all day.'

'Don't worry. Everything's going according to plan,' Charity laughed. 'I told you—we're doing our bit and the rest is up to you. You will be dining here and going back in the moonlight.'

'They'll be expecting us at the villa. They'll be worried.'

'No they won't. Dominique knows you're eating here.'

Stella watched as Charity bathed and fed little Tom and other members of the family prepared food and laid the table. With perfect timing Thomas and Adam arrived as everything was ready.

Stella noticed a conspiratorial grin exchanged by Thomas and his wife and felt a slight stab of envy as he kissed her and stooped to take the sleepy baby and put him to bed. Adam apologised profusely to Stella for his long absence and seemed somewhat bemused by Charity's calm acceptance of the situation.

'I thought you'd have been in trouble for being away all day,' he said to Thomas but the only answer was a broad grin.

As always, darkness fell quickly and in the lamplight the large family gathered round the table. Stella was seated next to Thomas who proved an attentive host and, assisted by the others, told her a lot about the island's food. After the meal, the younger members of the household cleared away while Charity and Thomas took Stella and Adam into the garden and gave them glasses of fruit punch which they said was made from an old island recipe.

'We'll have to think about getting back soon,' Adam said uneasily, looking at his watch. 'James will be wondering where we've got to.'

'He'll just think you've fallen into our unreliable ways.' Thomas laughed. 'Enjoy your drinks and I'll go and give the inside of the car a quick clean. It got rather dirty today and we don't want Stella to get oil on her dress.'

He departed, followed by Charity.

'I don't know what's got into those two today,' Adam commented. 'They don't usually behave like this. And I am really sorry that I haven't spent the day with you as I promised. There was so much I wanted to show you.'

'Never mind. I've had an enjoyable day here. Everyone is so happy it's quite infectious —and very relaxing.'

'This seems like the first time I've relaxed in days,' Adam said as he sipped his drink appreciatively. 'I wanted to talk to you but there's been so little opportunity . . .'

Stella waited, hoping, but he went on to tell her that his uncle thought it an excellent idea to found a scholarship in her father's name to be awarded annually to a pupil from the school where he had taught for so many years.

'I think that since the accident, my uncle has

developed a bit of a conscience and now admits that he maybe treated your father unfairly in the past. I suppose he feels this is a way of making amends.'

'Thank you very much. It's good to get that matter sorted out. I am really grateful to you.'

Despite her gratitude Stella felt acute disappointment. Surely if he had any feeling of love he would say something now, when time was so short. And he didn't look happy. Was it just tiredness, or was there something worrying him?

Of course, Charity would never know that the engagement to Nigel had never been a real one, but was she right in her belief about Adam's feelings? Her mind drifted over the events of the supposed engagement and the ring which she could never bring herself to wear and which she couldn't allow herself to sell either, and an idea occurred to her.

'I met a little boy here who says he's going into hospital to have his leg straightened. Charity said something about Janet sending some items to be sold.'

'Oh yes—the poor kid had a bad accident and it was believed nothing could be done for him. The "Reverend" who looks after the islands in this area is an American. He got a surgeon friend to come here and take a look and he says he can put it right if he operates soon.

'The islanders have set up a fund and Janet

has sorted out some items from the wrecks which the Reverend will sell on behalf of the fund. He's a real friend—practical as well as spiritual. He'll sell anything and get a good price in order to help.'

'Would he sell the ring your uncle gave me?'

'He would—but are you sure you want to part with it? It is quite valuable and we can't be sure that uncle wasn't telling the truth about it.'

'Knowing him as I do now, I don't believe he bought it for my mother—and even if he did, she would have been happy for it to be used to help a sick little boy.'

'Then it will give a welcome boost to the fund and I know they'll be very grateful.'

As he spoke Thomas came to collect their glasses.

'I'm sorry,' he said, 'but the car won't go.'

'It was running all right this afternoon,' said Adam in disbelief. 'There can't be much wrong.'

'I'll have a look in daylight,' Thomas said comfortably. 'But don't worry. We can use the boat. Charity wanted to go fishing anyway.'

Adam, a torch in one hand, held Stella's arm firmly with the other as she made her way gingerly along rickety boarding to the small boat where Charity was waiting. To Stella's surprise, it was Charity who steered the boat away from the shore while Thomas sat in the stern singing softly in his deep bass voice while the visitors were seated together in the centre.

'We often come out here,' Charity said. 'At home there are always family around and it's not easy to have a quiet discussion.'

'What she means,' Thomas put in, 'is that she doesn't like to throw things at me when my mother is around.'

'I'm sure Charity's not that bad.' Adam laughed.

'She has a terrible temper,' Thomas replied.

'We have frank discussions,' Charity said.

'I'm sure one of these days she'll put me out of the boat and tell me to swim home.' Thomas laughed.

While the banter went on, Stella looked up into the dark, spangled sky and watched the moonlight glittering on the water. Despite the hour the air was mild. It felt like a dream. Then she realised the boat was turning towards the shore and eventually Charity stopped the engine.

'This is as far as we go,' she said, a hint of laughter in her voice. 'I thought you were taking us to our jetty,' Adam protested.

'No. The water's quite shallow. You can carry Stella. It will be a pleasant walk along the sand and up the path at the end of the bay.'

'I never argue with my wife. I daren't,' Thomas said as Adam looked at him in bewilderment.

'When you are half-way up the path there's a big flat stone,' Charity said. 'Me and Thomas sorted out our differences on that rock. It's a good place to have a rest—the path is quite steep. Mind Stella doesn't slip.'

Adam stood up and the boat rocked alarmingly. With a laugh Thomas jumped out and steadied it.

'I'll take Stella ashore,' he said, 'otherwise she might get dropped in the water.'

Stella felt his muscular arms round her as he effortlessly carried her on to the white sand.

'I think Charity is giving Adam the benefit of her advice,' he whispered as he set her down.

A few seconds later Adam joined her, Thomas returned and they heard the engine start up.

'This is all part of a plot. Do you realise we've been set up?' he demanded, a mixture of laughter and bewilderment in his voice.

'I became more and more puzzled as the day wore on,' Stella admitted.

Adam put his arm round her as they floundered through the soft white sand.

'Their lives are simpler than ours.' He sighed. 'But they have a straightforward way of looking at things which we seem to have lost. Let's go as far as their magic rock and have a rest.'

As Charity had said, the path was steep and Stella felt quite breathless when they reached the flat rock and rested.

'I was attracted to you from the moment we

met,' Adam confessed at last. 'But it seemed to me then that you were involved with my uncle. I suppose he went out of his way to give that impression. And when jealousy got the better of me and I challenged you, how I wished I could have taken my words back!'

'And again, before Nigel left the island, he said you had told him you loved someone else. So I have tried to hide my feelings, but maybe I shouldn't have. Be straight with me, Stella. Who is this other man you told Nigel you were in love with? Someone you left at home and that you're planning to return to?'

Stella shook her head and laughed softly.

'No, Adam, It's nothing like that,' she whispered.

His embrace and murmured endearments left her in no doubt as to the strength of his feelings.

'But you told Nigel you loved someone . . .' he said at length.

'That was you,' she admitted.

'I can't let you go back with Janet and James,' he said at length. 'You must stay here with me. Thomas and Charity are planning a wedding already. They don't understand that you'll want to make your own plans—choose a dress . . .' his voice trailed off doubtfully.

'Charity has already made the dress—it's a picture,' Stella told him happily.

'Then will you let the Reverend marry us after Janet and James have left?'

She managed to agree before his lips met hers.

It was some time later that they rose stiffly from the rock to return to the villa.

'I've forgotten something,' Adam said, putting a hand into his pocket. To Stella's surprise he pulled out a torch, switched it on and waved it excitedly in the direction of the sea. From the darkness there was an answering flash and they heard the sound of a small engine starting up.

'Our wedding preparations are now in hand,' Adam said contentedly and hand in hand, they wandered on in the moonlight.

We hope you have enjoyed this Large Print book. Other Chivers Press or Thorndike Press Large Print books are available at your library or directly from the publishers.

For more information about current and forthcoming titles, please call or write, without obligation, to:

Chivers Large Print
published by BBC Audiobooks Ltd
St James House, The Square
Lower Bristol Road
Bath BA2 3BH
UK
email: bbcaudiobooks@bbc.co.uk
www.bbcaudiobooks.co.uk

OR

Thorndike Press
295 Kennedy Memorial Drive
Waterville
Maine 04901
USA
www.gale.com/thorndike
www.gale.com/wheeler

All our Large Print titles are designed for easy reading, and all our books are made to last.